The voice of Lao's teacher came back to her . . .

A swordsman knows his mind and weapon are one. Clear your mind and let your body do what it has been trained to do.

The Oriental blanked her mind now, and drew herself into a ball, balanced on her toes. When the enemy was eight feet away, Lao launched her body through the air, hands outstretched, fingers rigid. With the force of 120 hurtling pounds behind them, she became a human spear.

Her hands punctured the man's skin, ruptured intestine and snapped his spine.

The other members of the motorcycle gang watched in fascination as their buddy was torn apart by the small opponent.

The thugs froze in their tracks.

Mack Bolan's

ABLE TEAM

ABLE TEAM

Blood Gambit

Dick Stivers

A GOLD EAGLE BOOK FROM

WORLDWIDE

TORONTO · NEW YORK · LONDON · PARIS
AMSTERDAM · STOCKHOLM · HAMBURG
ATHENS · MILAN · TOKYO · SYDNEY

First edition June 1986

ISBN 0-373-61224-9

Special thanks and acknowledgment to
Tom Arnett for his contributions to this work.

Printed in Canada

PROLOGUE

"Remember, keep me in sight at all times," Winston Dangerfield murmured to his companions when they were alone on the elevator.

The two burly bodyguards looked at each other before saying, "Yes, sir." They kept the smirks off their faces, but not out of their eyes.

Dangerfield didn't need to look at them to know what they were thinking. He stared straight ahead at the elevator doors. As far as his guards knew, he was simply going to see Joshua Arma, chairman of the board and majority stockholder of Armageddon Arms Ltd. They believed nothing would happen to him inside an office where he had an appointment. They didn't understand a man like Joshua Arma, and Dangerfield was tired of trying to get through to them. He could only hope they were right and that he was simply getting paranoid.

When Winston Dangerfield's company, Binary Control Systems, went public, Armageddon Arms bought fifty-one percent of the stock. Suddenly Dangerfield found himself reporting weekly to old Arma, who somehow made him feel like a convict on parole. But this wasn't a regular meeting. The old shark had summoned him peremptorily to come and make a special report.

The elevator doors slid open at the thirteenth floor, the top floor. Dangerfield smiled dryly. Joshua Arma would never give ground to superstition by calling it the fourteenth floor. Followed by two alert bodyguards, the chief executive officer of Binary Control Systems stepped out of the elevator, his shoes sinking into the deep pile carpet of the executive floor.

In theory, Joshua Arma no longer ran his own company. His eldest son, Jude, was CEO. In practice, however, the old man kept an elaborate suite of offices on the executive floor and a remorseless finger on the pulse of the company.

Arma's secretary, a gorgon in her sixties, waved Dangerfield through to the inner sanctum. He rapped once on the large oak door and walked in, his guards close behind him.

Arma was speed-reading a thick technical report, turning a page every few seconds. In one corner of the office, an electrician stood on a ladder, working on a light fixture. Arma stuck a paper clip on the report to mark his place and looked up.

"Who the hell are they?" he demanded of Dangerfield, nodding in the direction of the bodyguards. His voice had the lilt of a Southern plantation owner from another era.

"You should be used to them by now," Dangerfield answered. "You see them every week."

"Well, son, familiarity ain't doing nothing for my sense of hospitality."

"I'm sorry, Mr. Arma, but they stay with me."

The old man waved the bodyguards to a sofa in a corner of his huge office.

"Sit down, Dangerfield. Tell Mr. Esenin how you're getting your tail in a knot, trying to promote the Little General."

Dangerfield hadn't noticed the man until now. The Binary chief turned to examine this new factor.

An underpaid accountant was Dangerfield's first guess. Esenin was a thin man of medium height. A few strands of dark hair were brushed sideways over his balding head. He wore a rumpled gray suit, a plain white shirt and a navy tie.

His eyes were dark brown and reminded Dangerfield of a snake's eyes. Esenin didn't bother getting up, but merely sat returning Dangerfield's stare.

Dangerfield carefully lifted the knees of his trousers as he sat down. He directed a questioning glance at the electrician.

"Don't you show no mind to Jones," Arma instructed. "The work has to be done. I trust him like I trust kin."

Dangerfield sized up the bald-headed man in coveralls on the ladder. He'd be ignored because Joshua Arma had said that they ignore him. Dangerfield felt he really must be getting paranoid; the electrician was about sixty and would probably have trouble managing a playful kitten.

Stalling for time, Dangerfield looked at Esenin and asked, "Exactly what would you like to know?"

"Why have you picked such an unusual way to promote your computer, and what do you think is standing in your way?"

"What do you know about the computer?"

"Suppose you begin by telling me what you feel I should know."

"What's your specialty, Mr. Esenin?"

"Making things happen."

Something in the precise dry voice told Dangerfield the question time was over. Also, he noted that the man spoke with an accent that he couldn't quite place. Dangerfield licked his lips before beginning.

"We've come up with a new miniature computer with a better power-to-weight ratio than ever before. We also have a RAM chip program that's a quantum leap in information handling and decision making. It's years ahead of any of our competitors. But the only contracts we've snagged are for two units that NASA will use in remote landing vehicles. The computer is much too good to waste by just sending vehicles over the surface of other planets.

"We've prepared a version that will fit in an oversize briefcase. We call it the 'Little General.' If Napoleon had had one, he would have won at Waterloo. It would have let Rommel trounce Patton in Africa. It has both the ability to handle details and the ability to generalize from incomplete facts. I haven't the slightest doubt that the Little General will elevate war to entirely new levels of sophistication."

"You new computer is terribly expensive, is it not?" Esenin asked.

"Hideously. The chips are produced by a process we can't automate. But how did you know?"

"It is logical. Both your government and mine are overly enamored of war toys. You would have sold a truckload by now if the computers were cheaper."

"Your government?"

"That is correct. I am a trade representative for the Soviet Union."

Dangerfield allowed just a hint of surprise to inflect his voice as he answered, "My company isn't allowed to sell computers to your country. The hi-tech freeze. I'm sorry."

"Oh, I have no intention of paying for one. You will give me one."

"What!"

Esenin smiled. "Mr. Arma will explain. But first finish your story. I take it that it is not easy to convince a government to spend a few million on an electronic general. I must congratulate you on your promotional idea. How did you think it up?"

Dangerfield turned to Arma. "Why are we discussing this with a Russian?"

A cherubic smile lit up Arma's round pink face. "Don't get lathered, son," he said in his Southern drawl. "Mr. Esenin insisted on this meeting as a condition to help us out of this mess you're getting us into. We're trying to find some way you can go ahead with this fancy promotion scheme of yours."

"If we don't proceed, Binary Control Systems will go bankrupt." There was ice in Dangerfield's voice.

"If you do go ahead as you plan, a lot of munitions firms will be bankrupt, and Armageddon Arms will probably take a whopping loss. I'm not about to let that happen." There was steel in Arma's voice.

"That doesn't make sense."

"It would if you used your head for more than a rest home for half-baked ideas. If the Western nations started using your Little General, would it give them an edge over Russia and her friends?"

"A hell of an edge," Dangerfield enthused.

"And Russia would have to pull in her claws?"

Puzzled, Dangerfield nodded.

Arma leaned across the desk, his green eyes blazing. "And when the Bear stops showing her fangs, where the hell are we going to sell our weapons?" he thundered.

The question stunned Dangerfield. He'd always considered weapons a form of security, never considering the other side of the coin—that insecurity was needed to sell those weapons. It was suddenly clear why the arms manufacturer was treating him like a backward schoolboy.

"So you want me to abandon the Little General?" Dangerfield's voice was perplexed and hurt, not yet angry.

Arma dismissed his question with a wave of his hand.

"Hell, son! We want to housebreak your 'coon dog, not give up huntin'. You invested a lot of time and effort in that machine. Now it's got to make you a profit. I just want you to do things so your profit isn't our loss.

"Besides, you ain't going to get to square one if you don't do something to save that promotion scheme of yours."

Esenin inserted himself smoothly into the conversation. "You have not as yet told me where you got your promotional idea. I thought it was excellent."

"Chess is the essence of war tactics and strategy," Dangerfield began. "I'm confident the Little General will beat the chess world's top masters, and governments will start buying like there's no tomorrow. So it seemed obvious to sponsor a tournament and invite the real achievers. A five-round Swiss-style event, with the Little General as one of the entries."

"But there are two problems," Esenin pointed out. "You must be certain that your computer and program can beat the international grand masters, and you have to persuade them to play the computer."

"I thought the purse would have been sufficient. Half a million dollars is one of the largest prizes ever offered in this type of tournament. The Little General would not be eligible for the prize money, whether it won or not."

"Actually, the Russian masters are frothing at the mouth to play in your tournament. I had to arrange for their acceptances to be delayed until we could reach an agreement."

"And no one's going to believe that contraption of yours is any good if it don't beat the Ruskies. Isn't that right?" said Arma.

Before he answered, Dangerfield watched the old electrician strip another wire. "That's right."

"So this meeting's about how to save your bloody company, not how to scuttle it."

"If you say so."

"Damned right I say so. Now, Mr. Esenin has a suggestion that just might kill two birds with one stone. If it works, it'll get them Russian chess piddlers to play your machine, and yet at the same time not kill the arms business dead."

Arma cast a glance at the two quiet, attentive bodyguards. "Just how completely do you trust them two fellows?"

"I trust them with my life, don't I?" Dangerfield answered brashly. He was secretly unsure: he had acquired the guards too easily since he'd sold two computers to NASA. He wouldn't be suprised if they reported to the government. It would be impossible to explain having discussed his technological breakthrough with a Russian. Certainly he couldn't continue the conversation in front of witnesses. But it was third down, and the opposition was rushing.

"I'd like to satisfy myself on that score, if you don't mind," Arma said. He beckoned to the two bodyguards. "You boys just mosey over here and talk to me for a minute."

The guards walked toward Arma's desk, their suspicions not aroused by the old man's politeness. They passed the electrician on the ladder but kept their eyes fixed on the munition manufacturer's beaming face.

From the ceiling tiles the electrician produced heavy cables that looked like giant automotive booster cables. With two hands he opened the first huge clamp and attached it to the head of the nearest bodyguard. The victim shook, stretched on tiptoe then fell forward.

The second bodyguard whirled. Horrified, he watched his friend's electric dance. Although his eyes were frozen by the sight, his hand darted for the Agent Special, carried in a belt holster. His hand never made it. A second huge clamp closed over his head, and he joined his fellow bodyguard in the dance macabre.

"What the hell are you doing?" Dangerfield demanded.

"I'd say he is eliminating a pair of government spies," Esenin observed calmly. "Colonel Caruthers Jones, I take it."

The electrician ignored the bodyguards' last spasms. "No one calls me Caruthers. Cannibal Jones, at your service."

Dangerfield groaned. He knew who Cannibal Jones was; he'd hoped never to meet the man. Colonel Jones had been court-martialed in Vietnam. According to the evidence, Cannibal and his crew had developed a taste for "fresh-toasted Gook," their elegant way of describing the flesh of Vietnamese they'd roasted with napalm. Hence the name Cannibal.

Some mysterious force had sprung the unit from a military stockade before death sentences could be delivered. Now its members accepted free-lance assignments as soldiers of fortune, rapidly acquiring a Robin Hood image although many people died horribly wherever Cannibal and his team appeared.

"You hired this man?" Dangerfield asked Arma.

"Hired him? Hell, he's worked for our little group ever since we helped him out of a tight spot."

"Your group?"

"You mean you didn't know? Where the hell have you been? I, sir, am chief executive officer of The Arms Group, a small lobby group interested in furthering the interests of those who wish to keep the world free."

Dangerfield licked his lips. "By that you mean the arms manufacturers."

"That's what I just said. Listen, damn it!"

Cannibal Jones removed the electrode clamps from the bodies and stored the clamps above the ceiling tiles. If he had disconnected them, Dangerfield hadn't noticed.

"I don't want any part of this," Dangerfield said a bit shakily.

"Tough," said Jones as he pulled up a chair to sit in on the conference.

"Without us, how will you account for the disappearance of your bodyguards?" Jones asked.

"*With* you, how will I account for the disappearance of my bodyguards?" Dangerfield countered.

"Nothing could be simpler, son," Arma said. "I've found you a couple of boys who look remarkably like those two." He gestured to the bodies on the plush red carpet. "They'll stick with you until the next shift shows up. Then they'll run like hell. All you need to say is that they told you they were substitutes for your regular guards, and you were too busy to check up on them. No one will be able to break that one."

"And when these bodies turn up?"

Jones laughed. It was a nasty laugh. "They never will."

Dangerfield shuddered.

"Let's get back to serious business," Arma said. "Here's how you're going to sell enough of those fancy computers to make us all rich."

Dangerfield was shaken, but not too shaken to reflect that Arma was already worth a half-billion dollars. What did he call rich?

"The computer you enter in the tournament is going to get hijacked by terrorists," Arma told Dangerfield. "It will happen just after the last day. So the world will know the results okay. Now, not only will that guarantee you all those Ruskie chess types will be there, but it will guarantee that none of them will beat your infernal machine. How does that suit you?"

Dangerfield knew it damn well better suit him, otherwise he stood a good chance of joining the two on the floor. Yet the carrot was as persuasive as the stick. Not only would the top Russian masters turn up, but also they'd be ordered not to beat the Little General. That would include the world champion and the two runners-up, which was enough to guarantee him all the sales he could handle for two years. He searched for a token objection. His life depended on not being sold too easily.

"I fail to see how this helps you with your problem."

The old man brushed away the comment as if it were an annoying fly. "That stolen computer is going to appear to be destroyed, but actually it will fall into Russian hands. You tell me what will happen to it."

"They'll duplicate it. In two years, every Communist nation in the world will be using a Little General clone!"

"Of course. But how many would you have sold to the Communists, anyway?"

"None. It's against the law."

"So, you see. You get lots of sales. You don't lose any sales you wouldn't have had in the first place. And the balance of power is maintained. We got the Little General. They've got something awful similar, which they'll claim to have invented themselves. And everyone keeps buying weapons. See, these things are easy to work out to everyone's advantage."

Dangerfield nodded glumly. He was going to be a rich man. Why did he feel as if he'd just been taken for a ride?

Esenin took up Dangerfield's conversion once more. "There is one other thing I need."

Dangerfield nodded, his stomach sinking.

"Just some spare parts that can be smuggled out in diplomatic pouches. They need not be anything sensitive. We shall destroy them when we obtain the Little General. Everyone will believe that the computer was destroyed. No one could possibly suspect you. You see how carefully we plan for your well-being?"

Dangerfield managed another glum nod.

"Be sure to supply convincing parts. It matters to my plan. Now, who else besides our comrades might beat your computer?"

"I really don't think any human can."

"What about Pescador?"

"You're well informed, Mr. Esenin. If anyone can, he can. He's not only the new U.S. champion, but also he's a computer programmer of no small ability. Every year we have a chess championship for computers only. This year Pescador is scheduled to play simultaneously against all the entries. I'll be at that demonstration to see how much of a threat he really is.''

"Is the Little General entered in that tournament?"

"No. We decided there'd be more suspense and press attention if it had never played chess in public before."

"Damn!" exclaimed Arma. "We got to be ready to do something if that son of a wetback turns out to be good."

"He can always be taken care of," Esenin suggested.

"I don't think so, sir," Arma rumbled in his Southern lilt. "If he comes down with fatal health, people are going to wonder who wanted him so poorly. We got to content ourselves just getting him out of the way until the tournament's over—'course it would be even better if he played that contraption and lost."

"What about a kidnapping?" Jones suggested. "My team could kidnap him and a few others, so no one would know who we really wanted out of the way. We could exchange the hostages for ransom, but by that time it would be too late to play in the Little General tournament."

"Sound idea, boy. An excellent plan. I can see you've got brains up there." Arma turned to Dangerfield. "If that boy looks too good, you tell me and I'll tell Colonel Jones here."

Then the old man turned back to Jones. "You won't do the job yourself because it might be associated with us. Hire the right men for the job. You got that?"

"If you say so, sir."

"I say so. I think we've covered all the bases, gentlemen."

Arma stood up. The others took their orders and marched. As he left the outer office, Dangerfield found two new bodyguards following him. He wasn't sure what terrified him the most: the idea that they wouldn't get away with this, or the fear that they would.

Walking between the two new guards, the soon-to-be-rich Dangerfield left Armageddon Arms, feeling like a condemned man.

1

"Be quiet!" Lao Ti snapped at Carl Lyons.

"I want him to tell me why he's wasting his time playing that stupid game against twenty-two computers at the same time."

Politician, leaning on a straight cane with a brass head, asked, "Why do you call chess a stupid game?"

Carl Lyons, called "Ironman" by the rest of Able Team, turned his frigid blue eyes on Rosario Blancanales, better known as "Politician," or just plain "Pol."

"You play the game; it must be stupid." Lyons's voice was curt.

Three feet away, Billy Pescador, United States chess champion, was poised in front of a chessboard, his hand hovering above a knight. His darkly tanned face showed that he found the antics of the three members of Able Team even more fascinating than his simultaneous exhibition against the best chess computer programs available.

"Could you save your argument until he finishes playing?" Lao suggested.

"If he's a good player, he won't mind an argument on the side," Lyons said.

Pescador's brown eyes sparkled, and he broke into a grin. He tossed back his collar-length black hair with a flick of his head. "You're right. But the programmers are waiting for me to make my moves. You must excuse me."

Turning his attention back to the chessboard, he quickly made a move, which the programmer entered into the computer. Pescador moved to the next board as the programmer made the chess move indicated by his computer.

The champion pondered for a few seconds, then his long, thin fingers swooped like a bird of prey, snatched up a bishop and moved it to an adjacent square. Without waiting for the programmer to enter the move, Pescador strode to the next board.

The boards and their corresponding remote computer terminals were arranged in a circle in a large banquet hall. Billy Pescador moved from board to board around the circle. Sometimes he motionlessly pondered a move for several minutes. Usually he needed only ten or twenty seconds to decide his play.

A woman with long blond hair, wearing war-surplus khaki fatigues, listened to the exchange between Lyons and Pescador with interest.

"If you think chess is so stupid, why do you want to go with the team to Dubrovnik?" she asked Lyons, who seemed startled by the question.

"We think you're going to need protection. That's our job."

"You defected at the last women's championship, didn't you?" asked Politician.

"I don't like the word 'defected.' It sounds as if I deserted or something. I escaped slavery. I'm Estonian. The Russians have moved into our country, taken over our government. We are no more than slaves in our own land. The Kurats have even tried to take away the name of our country, telling us we are now part of theirs." Her anger shone in her eyes.

Lyons grinned as he studied the woman. "I will never use the term defector again," he promised.

The sudden switch in his disposition surprised her. She looked up, locking her baby-blue eyes on his icy blue ones. "You're making fun of me?"

"He really isn't," Politician told her, defending his friend. He turned to Lyons. "Now smarten up, wise guy." He whacked him across the seat with his cane, a punishment that Lyons took calmly.

Politician was the oldest member of Able Team; his wavy hair was pure white, his skin deeply bronzed, his eyes black. At five foot eleven, he towered over the blond chess player, but he was still three inches shorter than Lyons. In his three-piece suit with its minute pinstripe, Rosario Blancanales looked like a prosperous banker.

"You're called Politician?" Her accent betrayed her Estonian background.

"That's right. And you're called Anne Harju."

Smiling, she continued to sort out the Able Team names. She gestured at Lyons. "Is he called Ironman because his manners are so rusty?"

Lyons let out a belly laugh.

Harju moved past Lyons to Lao Ti. "I'm Ann Harju. I've heard them call you Ti. Is that your name?"

Lao was an inch shorter than the female chess champion. The Oriental's dark eyes practically sparked when she said, "Yes, I'm Ti. But to you, I'm Dr. Lao."

"The other person called Gadgets—I don't see him," Harju said hastily.

"He's around someplace," said Lyons.

"I'm glad you're going to be around to protect us," said Harju. "You know, I would never go to a computer tournament in Russia, but Yugoslavia's different. It comes close to being a neutral nation. I'd hardly want to be snatched back by the Russians."

"We'll try to see that you're not," Politician told her, "but we have no reason to feel that you or any of the

American players are in special danger. We're simply an insurance policy."

"I wonder," Harju mused aloud.

"I don't like that waiter," Lyons said suddenly.

The others turned. Pushing a cart, a man in a hotel uniform was going around refilling pitchers of ice water around the room. He was an older man, stoop-shouldered, his hair brushed sideways to cover a shiny dome.

"What's wrong with him?" Harju asked.

Lyons didn't answer. He said, "I left something in the car," and strode suddenly to the exit. As he reached the doorway, several young men in leather jackets entered.

Watching Lyons leave, Anne Harju commented, "He is strange." Then she swung her head around and abruptly changed the subject. "Yeah, that's Winston Dangerfield!"

The man whom Harju had indicated exchanged a few words with the waiter tending water jugs then wandered toward the simultaneous exhibition.

He was as tall as Lyons and probably weighed thirty pounds more. He seemed fit, but unlike Lyons, didn't look as if his body had been welded out of steel plate. Tanned, he looked like a successful businessman.

"Who's Winston Dangerfield?" Politician asked.

"His company, Binary Control Systems, is sponsoring the tournament in Dubrovnik. They've put up $500,000 prize money."

"He must love chess," Lao said. She knew better but wanted to keep Harju talking.

Politician had left to find Gadgets. From the exhibition area came a programmer's groan when Pescador announced mate in five. The computer types looked grim as the champion strode from board to board. Only seven computers were still playing him.

"It's strictly business with him. He's entered his company's new computer in the tournament. It's a war computer. If it beats many masters, he'll sell enough to pay for the tournament okay."

"It's really two tournaments, isn't it?" Lao asked, her eyes fixed on the men in black leather who were wandering about the room.

"Yes, a men's tourney and a women's. I could use the $80,000 first prize. No women's tournament has ever had a first prize close to that."

"What are your chances?"

"Damn good."

"And Pescador's?"

"In the women's, I'm afraid he'd fail miserably. In the men's? Let me ask that guy over there." Harju turned and called to a blond man who was watching Pescador beat the computers. "Hey, Up. Come here for a minute."

The lean man, who looked about forty years old, strode over.

"What's so important I can't watch Billy finish?"

"One of our human Dobermans here wants to know Billy's chances in Dubrovnik."

The man called "Up" frankly studied Lao's small, delicately proportioned figure.

"You're Upton Quinn, Pescador's coach and second," Lao guessed.

He nodded. "Why do you want to know?"

"I'll tell you later," Lao answered. "Take Anne, collect Pescador and get them both under a table. Now."

Quinn studied her face. "Why?"

"Because a dragon is going to raise its ugly head. Now, go!" She shoved them toward the demonstration.

As they moved toward the chess exhibition, they looked over their shoulders at the small woman who had barked orders so unpredictably. Neither noticed the crew in black leather jackets, each member of which produced a handgun. They were staring at Billy Pescador, who was studying a chessboard, unaware of any threat.

Lao glided toward the nearest jacketed hood as if she didn't see the weapon in his hand.

"Get back or you'll get killed," the thug growled at her.

She carried no weapon but didn't slow her advance. Instead, she put a hand to her ear and grunted, "Huh?"

Standing at only five foot six and as thin as barbed wire, Lao seemed less threatening than a Girl Guide. But this thug had no intention of taking chances. He thumbed back the hammer on his Colt Commander and thrust the barrel toward her chest.

As his arm moved forward, he heard the cracking noise of a bone breaking. It had come from his own wrist. The small Oriental had slipped to one side as gracefully as a matador playing a bull and had administered a karate chop with lightning speed.

Lao had the automatic in her right hand. Her left shot up, straight as a spear. Fingertips penetrated flesh under the hinge of the jaw. The thug in black leather crumpled.

The leader of the gang barked, "Everyone against the wall. Last one there gets killed."

A finger tapped him on the shoulder and someone said, "Excuse me. You didn't say which wall."

The leader whirled. A man stood before him with his hands raised to shoulder height. One hand was wrapped around the center of a brass-headed cane. As the gunman pivoted, the cane spun to meet him. The brass head hit his temple with the sound of a mallet cracking a walnut. As the leader fell, Politician snatched the Ingram Mac-11 from his hand.

In another corner of the room, Gadgets Schwarz wiped his Gerber knife on another corpse before he resheathed it and picked up a Police Special from the floor.

"Where's Ironman?" Gadgets muttered. "He was the only one who bothered to come dressed." Dressed meant that Lyons's Colt Python rode its usual spot under his left arm.

The members of the Lucifers motorcycle gang didn't take long to figure out that something had gone wrong. This wasn't their first hired assassination; they considered themselves pros. If a couple of bystanders wanted trouble, they'd die slowly and painfully. The experienced Lucifers had a foolproof way to deal with white knights.

Each goon quickly grabbed a hostage to use as a shield.

"Throw down those weapons or these people will die!" one of them yelled.

LYONS HADN'T LIKED THE ASSIGNMENT from the word go. He liked it even less now. He'd told Yakov Katzenelenbogen, leader of Phoenix Force, just what he thought of spending his days with a bunch of effetes who had nothing better to do with their time but sit in front of sixty-four squares and push around carved pieces of wood. Actually, there was more to it than that. The assignment seemed too easy, and experience told him to suspect the easy ones.

Katz had ignored his protests. "When this comes down, they may really need protection," the Israeli had said. "We just don't know what the Russians will do when two of their best defect at once."

"And we're supposed to go to Yugoslavia and escort these red turncoats back?"

"That's the picture. They'll leave with you right after the tournament."

"Why not before?"

"They want their chance at the half-million in prize monies."

"Bloody tax dodgers."

Katz shook his head. ''In the Soviet Union they live like sports stars do here. They'll be facing a drop in life-style and lose the adulation of the crowds. In the United States, people don't think much of chess. In other countries, it's as big a draw as soccer.''

''Then why are they defecting?''

Katz didn't answer or argue. No one won a debate with Ironman when he smelled something wrong.

Lyons took a swig of his coffee. It was cold. In the field he wouldn't have noticed, but this was Stony Man, and he was being given an assignment that went outside Able Team's antiterror expertise. He threw the mug across the room and watched it shatter on the wall.

Katzenelenbogen didn't blink. He kept his calm dark eyes fixed on Lyons. He knew he had the Able Team leader as soon as he asked the inevitable question.

''Why us?'' Lyons demanded.

''There's no way to brief you on this one. Yugoslavia's Communist, but not strongly under Russian control. It's dependent on the West for tourists and huge bank loans. Otherwise, Binary Control Systems would never get a permit to take its new computer there. The defectors will be good propaganda. Both the U.S. team and the computer may need protection. We have no pull in Yugoslavia. So we can't supply backup. Who else are we going to send to play it by ear?''

''You're right,'' Lyons told him.

''What?''

''It sucks.''

He got up and left the room to break the news to the rest of the team.

WHEN HE LEFT THE HALL where Pescador was playing the computers, Lyons deliberately plowed through the newcomers. He shouldered four of them out of the way, satisfying himself that they were all wearing guns.

He went straight to the car Able Team had rented at the airport. He pulled the baggage from the trunk and dumped it all on the back seat and rummaged through the piles of clothes for guns and spare clips. He didn't have to dump his own bag; whether he was off duty or not, he knew exactly where his weapons were.

He strapped on Politician's silenced Beretta 93-R. It was a good weapon in a crowd. There was little danger of one of its subsonic bullets passing through one body to kill some innocent. He didn't bother with Gadgets's Ingram because he was sure the electronics specialist would be armed by the time Lyons returned to the hall. He took Ti's short-barreled Heckler & Koch MP-5, throwing some spare clips in his pocket. Last of all, he threw his Konzak assault shotgun over his shoulder and turned back to the hotel.

Lyons attracted a stir in the lobby. He had the awesome shotgun over his shoulder, the 93-R in his right hand and the MP-5 in his left. The pockets of his sport jacket bulged with spare magazines. Dead silence fell as he stalked to the banquet hall.

Lyons arrived at the door to the hall to find that the gang members were grabbing hostages. Lao spotted Lyons standing in the doorway. When a hostage taker demanded that Able Team surrender its weapons, Lao threw the Colt Commander in a high arc, straight at him. The thug grinned and stepped to one side, forcing his hostage, an elderly woman, to do a fast shuffle to keep from falling.

As Lao released the gun, Lyons launched her own weapon to her. All eyes in the room were riveted on the soaring Colt Commander. A few switched to follow the flight of the MP-5.

The punks were expecting trouble from Gadgets and Pol, and the flying gun made them temporarily forget to watch their backs. Lyons snapped down the front handgrip of the 93-R. With the two-handed grip on the silenced gun, Lyons lined up the sights on the first goon's head and squeezed off a single shot. No one noticed the Beretta's polite cough, but one hostage wondered what had happened when his captor suddenly collapsed.

Lyon swung to the next target. He didn't like it. Too many innocents in the line of fire. He skipped that one and swung on to another head that was silhouetted against the bare wall. Another cough, another released hostage.

Politician and Gadgets scrambled to one side. The barking of handguns chipped plaster over their heads.

Gadgets lined up on an exposed leg. The Police Special didn't have a polite cough; it had a short bark. One would-be assassin fell to the floor, dragging his male hostage with him. The captive had enough sense to tuck himself into a ball, giving Gadgets a clear head shot. The next .38 mashed an eyeball into the killer's brain.

Politician glanced over to make sure Pescador was safe. He had noticed the gang members eyeing the chess champion and was sure Pescador was the main target. To the warrior's horror, he saw the chess player still standing by a chessboard, as though ignorant of the gun battle around him.

One goon was trying to use the confusion to line up a shot on Pescador. Politician ruined the killer's aim with three bullets in the chest.

Then Politician sprang to his feet and dashed into the crowd. He placed himself between two gang members who were too deep in the mob to be safely shot. He lunged with his cane, as if making a sword thrust, crushing an Adam's apple. Then he whipped the brass cane head over and back, snapping a gun wrist as if it were a dry twig. The gunsel howled and turned into the upswing of the cane. The impact crushed his skull.

Lao caught her MP-5 in her right hand and chambered a cartridge with her left. Her fire perforated two leather jackets. Then she, too, leaped into the crowd to get a goon who was still protected in the throng of innocent bodies.

As Lao closed in on her target, the chess player he'd seized let his legs go limp, pulling the captor forward. Lao used a right-hand strike that drove the gun barrel into the top of the man's skull.

The bystanders in the room looked at each other in silent amazement when they realized that no one but the gunmen had been hurt.

Over the stunned silence, Pescador told the programmer cowering under the table, "Please come back and register my next move. It's checkmate!"

Lyons groaned to himself. How were they going to keep those chess idiots alive?

2

"What the hell are we doing here?" Upton Quinn demanded.

The van emerged from a long driveway between rows of grapevines. Ahead of them spread a cross-shaped mansion with an accumulation of wings and additions that dated back to the 1920s. Although the building was done in many architectural styles, it was unified by an air of relaxed elegance.

As they drove around the house, the occupants of the van saw a large, rectangular swimming pool, a generous sun deck, and more vineyards. Ahead, a double row of bush flanked a small river. Rows of trees broke the vineyard into smaller sections. Everything had the lush green of a friendly April.

"Looks like a bloody prison," Anne Harju remarked.

Lao Ti, who had been absorbing the beauty and elegance of the setting, snapped her head around.

"How so?"

"It's like the Soviet Union," Harju explained in an angry voice. "If you're good at chess or sport, you get very comfortable, elegant places to train. Try to leave and you get trouble. Beautiful, but a bloody prison just the same."

"This time it's for your protection," said Gadgets from the fourth and final row of seats in the van.

"That's what I've always been told," Harju said.

"How far are we from town?" Pescador asked.

"Calistoga is about three miles farther," Politician answered from the driver's seat.

"Ah, yes, Calistoga," Quinn said, imitating W. C. Fields. "A town of four thousand souls. Very quiet place, and very boring. I spent a month there one weekend last year."

Politician brought the van to an abrupt halt then turned and said, "End of the line. Everyone out."

Lyons, who had said nothing during the entire trip from Monterey, stalked off, evidently to inspect the building and grounds.

The others climbed out more slowly, stretching and looking around. The setting seemed to subdue the four members of the chess team.

"Is this a winery?" asked Tom Kerr, a black chess player.

Politician answered, "Right. Some friends of mine own it and take in guests. This is too early for the tourist season, so we have the place to ourselves."

"Great. All we really need is to live like monks," Pescador said.

"It's not that bad."

"Worse," Pescador answered.

Lunch consisted of cold cuts, fresh-baked bread, fruit and a light sparkling wine, but the way Pescador and Harju complained, it might have been sawdust.

Quinn kept grumbling about the lack of beer until even the chess players ignored him. Harju started calling Lyons "commandant." Pescador tried to persuade Gadgets of the hopelessness of the operation. "There are too many concealed approaches. The place is practically indefensible."

"True," Gadgets agreed.

"Then why are we here?"

"To keep you from being killed."

"But you just admitted the place is indefensible."

"We're not here to defend the place, just a few spoiled chess players. The main defense is that no one knows where you are."

Pescador shook his head. "We can't hide. We need people to train with. Who's going to come to this place? Chess players are urban rats."

"What about training with a computer?" Lao asked.

Quinn laughed scornfully.

Harju shook her head. "You think that would work? It won't. Computers can play only to the expert level. That's a long way from being a master. You saw Billy beat twenty at once, didn't you?"

"Those were amateur programs. I'll make you a professional package."

"You know that much about chess?" Pescador asked, genuinely curious.

"I know little about chess, but I know a lot about computers and programming. I'll borrow the best and improve it."

Pescador smiled and shook his head. "I'm a programmer, too. And I have a special interest in chess. I'm afraid you've got too simple a view of the problem."

Lao said, "I'll make a wager."

Upton Quinn grinned. "This should be easy pickings. What do you have in mind?"

"You three stay here for one week and answer my questions fairly. Then Billy plays my program. If the program wins, you continue to train with the computer where we can keep you safe. And you let us tend to security at the tournament site."

"And if Billy wins?"

"We'll go where you say and try to keep you alive. Plus, I pay each chess player $3,000 for your wasted time."

"Hold it!" Politician interrupted. "You're offering $9,000 against a week of their time."

"Your mathematics is excellent," Lao answered.

"But the odds are heavily against you."

"Your odds-making is abominable," Lao said.

Politician shrugged. "It's your money."

"Correct. Two out of three isn't bad."

Politician gave up.

"Done!" Quinn yelled triumphantly.

"Wait," Pescador interrupted. "I'm the one who has to play her program." He turned to Lao. "What rules?"

"Same rules you'll be using in the Dubrovnik tournament. Anne can be the tournament director. I'll abide by her decisions."

"That's no good. I stand to make $3,000 out of this," Harju objected.

"You'd sell your honesty for $3,000?"

Harju laughed. "Okay. I judge."

"You're sure you won't regret this?" Pescador asked the small Oriental.

"Do you regret a good battle if you lose?"

The chess champion nodded. "Okay, done. What do you want to know?"

"Just two things, right now. Who has the best program and what chips will I need?"

Pescador scratched his chin. "Not as easy to answer as I thought. The best program to date is Belle from Northern Labs. It just made a master rating. Binary Control System has the Little General. They've let it be known that it has much better microprocessors. No one knows how good the program is, and I'm sure they're not going to tell."

"Okay," Lao answered, turning her attention back to the food.

The rest followed her example.

That afternoon she tied her computer into the telephone lines and settled down to make things happen. She made her connections through Kurtzman's computer at Stony Man.

Requests placed through Brognola at the White House brought immediate response from the scientists who had developed Belle. The program was sent through the telephone lines, and Lao had it in her computer before dinnertime.

Cooperation from Binary Control Systems was much slower, but Dangerfield agreed to talk to her if she came to his office in San Jose. She made an appointment for the next day then telephoned Brognola and discussed the situation with him.

After dinner she and the players discussed the theory of chess and war, which are practically identical. To prepare for a tournament, chess players study the most recently published games of their opponents, and Lao learned where to find these.

That night she phoned Stony Man once more and arranged for the air force to deliver a library of chess publications and an optical scanner for her computer. Her contact at Stony Man promised the required materials would be delivered the next day.

Lao turned in about ten-thirty, content that she had done what she could for the day. The chess players, who were athletes in training, had already turned in. The last thing they discussed was what they'd do with their imminent windfalls of $3,000.

"WHY THE HELL WOULD good mercenaries stay at a crummy hotel like this?" the huge man asked Cannibal Jones.

Cannibal waited until Francis Fatheringham, known to his teammates as Feces, unfolded himself from the front seat of the van. Feces stood six foot six and weighed 320 pounds. His round face had a healthy flush, and his blue eyes were more innocent than those of a newborn baby. His pinstripe was custom-tailored to Feces's tremendous size; it had set

Cannibal back a thousand bucks. Now the innocent-looking giant looked more dependable than the pope. The effect was worth it.

Doris Drane moved from behind the wheel. She attached herself to Cannibal's arm as she joined Feces in dubious appraisal of the hotel.

"L.A.'s such a crummy town," she commented. "Why would mercenaries stay in a crummy joint like this? You'd think they'd find enough fleabags when they were in Africa or someplace."

As they walked into the run-down lobby, Feces's deep booming voice filled the cramped lobby. "This is close to a merc bar where mercs go to pick up assignments, plus it has great jazz, the prices are much lower than the swankier places, and above all else, this place is right in the middle of hooker heaven."

The desk clerk scowled at the huge man but smiled weakly when the big man glanced that way.

Cannibal knew the room numbers. They went straight to the elevator.

In the elevator Drane asked, "Why didn't we bring Slaughter and O.D.?"

"That wimp Dangerfield thinks he may have a lead to the chess types. They stayed to check it out. We don't need the full gun team to handle a dozen mercs."

Shaughnessy O'Hearn and his eleven associates had taken over one wing of the seventh floor. But there was no sign of life there—for a simple reason. Ten in the morning was not considered a fit hour for a soldier of fortune who had whiled away the night, first in a bar frequented by mercenaries and those seeking to hire them, then in the arms of ladies available for $100 a night.

Doris Drane consulted a slip of paper in her purse. "O'Hearn's in 717."

Feces squinted at room numbers in the dim light of the corridor. When he found 717, he raised his large booted foot and slammed it into the door, near the lock. The door jamb splintered, and the security chain snapped.

The sandy-haired man in the bed bounced to his feet and grabbed a Colt 1911 from the night table. His hired lady, a thin, worn creature with long black hair, was much slower gathering her wits.

As quick as O'Hearn had been, it was not fast enough. Lashing out with his foot, Feces smashed the automatic from the merc's fist. Then he wrapped one huge paw right around the mercenary's thin neck.

The lady screamed. Cannibal grabbed her hair and forced her back on the bed. He closed his teeth around her throat.

"One squeak and he'll bite your throat right out," Drane told the prostitute. Her voice couldn't have been more casual if she had been discussing the weather.

The woman's eyes went wide with shock and pain from the teeth digging into her windpipe. There was no scream. When he felt her body go limp, Cannibal released her and straightened up. He looked toward Drane, who was behind the door.

The noise had not escaped notice. The sound of several doors opening along the hall was followed by the sound of feet running in the carpeted hallway. Three tough-looking guys appeared in the doorway with handguns. One, wearing a beard, had taken the time to put on pants; the other two wore only underwear. "Come in, gentlemen," Cannibal told them. "I was about to make Mr. O'Hearn an offer you can't refuse."

"Just get your hands in the air."

Cannibal didn't raise his arms; Feces did. The difficulty was that the huge thug still had one hand wrapped around O'Hearn's neck. The sandy-headed man kicked and croaked like the guest of honor at a lynching.

"Come in," Cannibal repeated. "You'd better not shoot accidentally. I'd hate for my friend's death spasm to accidentally break Shaughnessy's neck."

The trio hesitated; Cannibal Jones snapped out one word, "Now!" Then they quickly obeyed.

When they were in the room, Drane spoke from behind the door. "Now, men—and I do see that you are men—place your weapons on the floor."

The short curvaceous woman with the golden hair and innocent blue eyes was covering them with an unusual-looking gun that had a nine-inch barrel and an overhead drum as big around as the length of the gun.

"What the hell is that?" asked one mercenary, more curious than frightened by the odd weapon.

"It's the short version of the AM180. I can turn all of you into chopped dog meat in less than half a second."

The three mercenaries paled and set their weapons on the floor.

"That's better," Feces boomed. He lowered the terrified O'Hearn to the floor.

Cannibal scooped the weapons and moved them to the far corner of the room. Then he sat on the rumpled bed and absentmindedly stroked the terrified prostitute's thigh.

"Shall we talk business?" he asked O'Hearn.

The mercenaries were shaken, and their near nakedness did nothing to bolster self-confidence. They smarted from the contemptuous ease with which they'd been handled.

O'Hearn nodded at the prostitute. "What about her?"

Cannibal Jones glared at the merc leader. "I wouldn't want her getting the rest of your men all worked up."

"Yeah. Well, what do you want?"

"A kidnapping."

"Some backwater head of state. We've done that before."

"It's not that. We want a buy-back arranged. And you can keep whatever money comes from it."

"That gets trickier. Kidnapping's easy enough. But getting away with the ransom is as tricky as hell. Where is this supposed to take place?"

"Possibly right here in California."

"Here! And who are the intended victims?"

"No politicians. Just some chess players."

O'Hearn relaxed. "Who the hell would pay money for chess players?"

"The United States Chess Federation. Both the men's and women's champions will be in the scoop."

"You're nuts. It would take an organization weeks to come up with serious bread."

"That's what we thought."

"If you want them out of circulation, why don't you simply have them iced?"

"We are instructed to enact a kidnapping. It's easier."

"Why don't you hotshots do it, if it's so easy?"

"We follow orders. You do the same."

"You won't do the job for a simple reason. It stinks."

Cannibal Jones was not in the least interested in O'Hearn's objections. He knew he had the trash of the mercenary world. He pulled some bundles of currency from a pocket of his tweed jacket.

"Here's fifty thousand reasons now, and you'll get another fifty thou when the idiots are returned, plus whatever reasoning power you can extract from the Chess Federation."

O'Hearn's eyes lit up but he tried to appear uninterested. "What sort of reasoning power has this Chess Federation got?"

"Practically none but their magazine appeal could launch a very large subscription fund."

"That could take months."

"Give them exactly three weeks," Drane said from where she still covered the mercenaries with her .22 machine pistol. "Time your demands to coincide with their publication date, so they can work an appeal into their magazine. I've written out the schedule for you." She reached into a pocket of her safari shirt and produced a folded piece of paper that she tossed to the floor.

O'Hearn looked at the bundle of money that Jones had dropped between the prostitute's legs. "I guess we could take your down payment and split."

"Where to?" Jones asked.

"Don't worry, we'll be there," O'Hearn hastened to assure him.

"I'm not worried. I know you'll take care of all the loose ends."

O'Hearn reached for the money. "I didn't really want to do this," he said, thumbing through the bills.

"You enjoyed it when you were IRA," Jones commented. "I'll call you tomorrow with the location of the chess players."

With that, the three Armageddon enforcers backed out of the room.

3

Ivan Esenin leaned across the borrowed desk and fixed the small man with his coldest glare. They were in Sofia, Bulgaria, and the desk had been borrowed from Esenin's counterpart in the Durzhavna Sigurnost, the most vicious secret police in the Soviet bloc.

Esenin broke his stare with a yawn.

The small man on the other side of the desk met Esenin's cold stare without flinching. Stefan Barazov, known throughout the terrorist world as "the Shrew", had not built his reputation for effective terrorism by shrinking from anyone, not even his KGB bosses.

Standing five foot four and weighing 135 pounds, Barazov bore a striking resemblance to Napoleon Bonaparte, a resemblance heightened by his dark hair, which he wore short and brushed straight forward. His smooth olive complexion and doe-brown eyes with long lashes made him seem almost effete to men and yet irresistible to women.

His voice divided the sexes even more radically. The soft rasping voice stirred female hearts with thoughts of romance and male hearts with the chill of a deadly snake. No man who heard Barazov speak doubted the small Bulgarian's ability to lead the most implacable and violent terrorists in the world.

"If I yawned," Esenin said, "it is because I was on the west coast of America yesterday. I flew here especially to give you your instructions. Tomorrow I shall be back there."

"Halfway around the world and back just to give me my instructions. I am impressed."

"Good. I shall tolerate no mistakes in this operation. My career depends on the results of this one operation. So you can be sure that your life hangs on its success."

"Perhaps if we moved from the threats to the planning, things would have a better chance of working out," Barazov said.

"There is to be a chess tournament in Dubrovnik. It is being sponsored by an American firm that will enter a computer as one of the contestants."

"The Little General, I believe. And you want it."

"How did you know?"

Barazov's smile was a half sneer. "Anyone who follows chess knows of the tournament. It has aroused much speculation. And of course, the Russians always want American computers."

"We like to know how they are progressing."

"Of course. If the Russian scientists did not know how the Americans were progressing, Russia would have no computers at all."

"I am in no mood for your cynicism. If you feel that way, why not work for the Americans?"

"I have considered it, but I am not particularly fond of working in Central America. Still, it would be better than taking this assignment inside the Warsaw Pact. When I kill Americans, I am a hero of the socialist state. When I kill members of a socialist republic, I am a dead criminal. Besides, with all your elaborate build up, I take it you have a few more complexities to add."

"Yes, we must save face all around. This must embarrass the Soviet Union as much as it does anyone."

Barazov grinned and waited for an explanation.

Esenin leaned back, feeling secure. He knew his plan was foolproof. All he had to do was lay it out. Barazov might be as vain as a peacock, but he was competent. He would appreciate the sound planning.

"We will allow the tournament to draw to a close. When things seem to be finished, Yugoslav security will relax as much as it ever relaxes. At that point, you move in with a large force, grab the computer and kidnap a couple of the Russian players."

"Is that when Russia becomes embarrassed?"

Esenin squinted at Barazov. Was that damn Bulgarian laughing at his plan? He decided not. Even Barazov would not put his neck that far out on the chopping block.

"No. One of the players you kidnap will be grand master Igor Kubasov. Anyone else you take will manage to escape, but Kubasov will be killed, and the computer will be hit by a mortar."

Barazov raised his eyebrows. "Kubasov? Whose ass did he fail to kiss?"

"You are becoming tedious," Esenin warned.

"Then I had best be careful that I am not one of the sacrificial goats to be left behind. That might really embarrass the Kremlin."

"Yes. Be careful. To answer your question, Kubasov has become dispensable. To have Spassky play for France has caused discomfort in high circles. Kubasov has always been outspoken. His wife died a month ago—"

"And you can no longer trust him not to defect, because the man's such an egotistical bastard that he's close to no one. So there's no one to hold as hostage when he's out of the country," Borazov finished.

Esenin didn't waste breath by denying the situation. Barazov knew the reality of life within the Warsaw Pact countries. Esenin understood where Barazov was coming from. The terrorist's idealism had disappeared long ago, but the taste for suffering had grown into an obsession. Barazov continued to serve the Soviet Union only because doing so gave him the maximum opportunity to express his lust for violence and death. The man was a touch too intelligent, perhaps, and sometimes exasperating, but he was immensely useful, nonetheless.

"I take it I'll be supplied with a dummy computer to burn away?"

Esenin nodded. "How did you know?"

"Typical KGB overcomplexity. What about the Americans?"

"Don't liquidate or kidnap them unless they get in the way. The computer will be America's embarrassment. It would be best if dead chess masters were confined to the Soviet Union. But there is the current women's champion of the United States—a traitor. It would be gratifying if she stayed behind to stand trial."

"Someone should see she 'volunteers' to be repatriated. What about Pescador? I hear he'll be a greater embarrassment to the Soviet Union."

"Unfortunately Pescador is going to meet with an accident before he leaves for Yugoslavia."

"Then the botched shoot-out at the computer tourney in California was your masterpiece?"

Esenin's voice was as frosty as Siberia. "I have no need of your sarcasm, Barazov. Even the American hoodlums are incompetent. It is a mistake that I must return to America to remedy."

"The hoodlums may be incompetent, but whoever took care of them wasn't. Watch yourself, Esenin."

"This is a new development! You're concerned for my welfare?"

Barazov stood up. His grin was frostier than even the KGB agent's. "Of course. I haven't been paid yet. I expect to be paid double for working in Yugoslavia."

Esenin nodded. He remained seated, clenching and un-clenching his fists as Barazov strode out.

IT WASN'T A LONG DRIVE from Silklands Winery near Calistoga to the Binary Control Systems' offices in San Jose. Lao Ti covered the distance in three hours in a rented Corvette. As she pulled into a parking lot, she glanced at her watch; she had five minutes until her appointment time. She climbed out of the car and began to walk toward the building.

The parking lot attendant wasn't sure there was space for another visitor's car. He yelled, "Take that car away or I'll have it towed away!"

Lao answered, "When you've parked it, deliver the keys to me in Dangerfield's office."

Then she continued to the building, ignoring the attendant's ranting.

The tall executive rose when Lao was shown into his office. He strode around his desk with his hand outstretched.

"Dr. Lao, it's a pleasure. I've followed your career with interest after you moved from Japan to California. However, I lost track of you somehow. What are you doing now?"

"Hunting terrorists."

"Seriously."

"Seriously. But I do wish to put together a chess program. I understand that BCS has made a breakthrough."

Dangerfield gestured Lao to a chair then sat down. He answered, "We have. The computer is primarily designed to make war decisions. Chess is merely an abstracted form of generalship. We're sure that our Little General will knock the boots off 'em. You've heard about the tournament, of course."

Lao nodded. "I'd like some of the giant chips you're using in Little General."

Dangerfield grinned. "So would a lot of other people."

Lao grinned back. "There are two differences. One: this is a government project. Two: you'll make an exception for me."

"Why would the government want a chess computer?"

"To enable the American players to practice in private. We'd simply buy a Little General, but I have a feeling it won't be available until after your tournament."

"In that, you're right. Surely you don't expect to duplicate the Little General before then?"

Lao shook her head. "We only want to give the players a chance to stay in shape. Whatever we give them will be a patch-up job."

"I still don't see why you're so sure I'll help. You haven't convinced me that this is in my own best interest."

There was a light tap on the office door, and Dangerfield's secretary entered with Lao's keys. "The guard on the lot brought these for Dr. Lao."

Dangerfield waved her away. "Give the keys to Mr. Smith," he told his secretary. "When Dr. Lao's ready to leave, I'll phone him to bring the car to the door."

When the office door was closed once more, Dangerfield returned to his visitor. "Well, Dr. Lao, you can appreciate that releasing proprietary material is apt to negatively affect our bottom line. I see no reason to risk a flub like that."

"You'll need an exit permit to take your computer to Yugoslavia. It's part of the Warsaw Pact."

"Only nominally. It's really a neutral nation."

Lao ignored his argument. "If your Little General's to travel legally, you'll supply me with chips in return for my word that they won't be used for commercial purposes. Otherwise, you don't have a hope of taking one of your computers to that tournament."

"You have that sort of pull?"

"Phone the White House. Ask for Mr. Brognola."

"The White House? Do you have the number?"

"Yes, but you'll be better convinced if you get the number yourself."

He picked up his telephone. "You're bluffing."

Lao merely smiled.

Ten minutes later, Dangerfield hung up the telephone and looked speculatively at Lao.

"Okay," he said. "What do you need?"

"A couple of the CPU chips and a full complement of compatible RAM chips."

"And how many of our ROM chips?"

"None. I'm not after secrets, merely hardware."

Dangerfield used the telephone to request the parts then said to Lao, "I didn't believe you when you told me that before."

"That's your problem."

"You wouldn't want to change jobs, by any chance? I'm damn sure I can pay you more than the government."

Lao stood up, shaking her head. Dangerfield said, "Well, if you change your mind you know where I am." He snatched the telephone. "Smith? Bring Dr. Lao's car around, please."

The CEO of Binary Control Systems stood up and smiled. He offered to buy Lao lunch someday, and she politely accepted. Then the secretary brought in a small box of computer parts; Dangerfield checked the contents and handed them to Lao.

"Do be careful. If our competitors get their hands on these little babies, it will ruin us."

"You have my word. Thank you."

Lao walked from the office, finding her own way to the front door.

SLAUGHTER SMITH LEANED BACK and put his feet on the large desk, empty except for a telephone. He grinned at the ebony-skinned pilot who was sprawled out in a visitor's chair with his shiny boots on another.

"See O.D. I told you being an executive was a snap."

For Slaughter, who usually confined himself to an occasional grunt, that was a long speech. O.D. shook his head and squinted at his fellow member of Cannibal Jones's team. Slaughter was a six-foot bean pole topped with a head of unmanageable red hair.

"What's got your pecker up?" O.D. asked in his usual British accent.

"Here we sit, keeping warm, while the others risk their balls in an airplane. Sure beats flying."

"I like flying," the black pilot reminded the weapons and explosives expert.

"Yeah. But you're too far out of it to know the difference."

O.D.'s eyes narrowed to slits. "Were you intending to make something out of it?"

To the relief of both, the telephone rang. Slaughter Smith snatched the receiver.

"Yeah?... This is Smith... Okay." He hung up.

"What was that?"

"Work. Dangerfield's secretary has some car keys. We're to pick them up and bring Dr. Lao's car to the front door."

O.D. swung his legs down. "From executive to parking lot attendant. You sure know how to come down in the world."

"Shut up," Smith growled as he opened the door of the borrowed office.

Smith's idea of executive dress was a pin-striped dark-blue suit, a narrow knit tie and a white shirt. But any business-like effect was diminished by his cowboy boots, white Stetson and large silver belt buckle.

Orville Daemeus Yus, known to his face as "O.D." and behind his back as "Odious," made no such concessions to custom. He wore a brown denim shirt, pants and a jacket of shiny black leather, congress boots and a brown cap with a black plastic visor. Few had the courage to get close enough to notice that the edge of the visor held a row of razor blades.

The parking lot attendant wasn't quite sure where the two strange dudes fitted in the company hierarchy, but he was sure he'd cooperate with them. He pointed out Lao's rented Corvette then took the coffee break the two men suggested.

Slaughter produced a small homing device. He worked it into a black tacky substance and pressed it inside the left rear wheel well. When he straightened up he nodded to O.D. They went over to a van parked close to the entrance to the lot. A quick check of the electronic gear in the van indicated that the homing device was working perfectly.

"Fifty-mile range. We can't lose this doctor character," Slaughter grunted.

They drove the sports car to the front door and waited. A few minutes later, a diminutive Oriental, wearing jeans and a plaid shirt and holding a small box under her arm, stepped off the elevator. It took Smith several seconds to catch on that he was looking at Dr. Lao. By then she was beside the car. He rushed out and offered the keys.

"Dr. Lao?"

Nodding, she took the keys.

He held the car door then stood uneasily while she looked him up and down. When she had slipped in behind the wheel with the box beside her, he closed the door.

"Thanks," she said.

Then she took off, peeling rubber.

Slaughter and O.D. watched her go. When the car disappeared around a corner, they climbed into the van. Slaughter said, "That bitch is going to lead us right to those chess players. And when she does, I'm going to take special delight in taking care of her myself."

O.D. just laughed.

4

Ivan Esenin couldn't remember the name of the youth who was driving the car. The KGB agent didn't care sufficiently to ask. It was enough that young radicals gave support to KGB efforts when needed. Who they were didn't matter. Few stayed with the party into middle age, when they could be really useful.

Esenin did remember his cover story. That mattered. A good agent never asked sympathizers to help with theft, sabotage and murder. Instead the operative asked for help in righting some type of wrong.

According to his present story, he was trying to find chess players who had been kidnapped by Binary Control Systems, because they knew that the Little General had first been developed and displayed in Russia. Esenin had convinced his driver and several cohorts that the advances in computer engineering being made by BCS were at the expense of the Russian inventors, robbing them of their patent protection. The agent wasn't sure why the young Americans would accept such a ridiculous story, but he knew before he used it that it was exactly the type of story that would keep his inexperienced helpers enthusiastic.

When Slaughter Smith and O.D. Yus emerged from the BCS building, Esenin's mental mug file clicked into place. When he had discovered Cannibal Jones and his crew were involved, Esenin checked their files. His careful preparation was paying off, as usual. Esenin watched something being planted on a Corvette. He couldn't tell whether it was a bug or a bomb.

To the KGB agent, it was logical to watch Binary Control Systems. If an American computer and American players were involved in the same tournament, Esenin assumed the two parties would decide beforehand which was to win; that was how it would happen in the Soviet Union. He didn't believe the bullshit old Arma had handed him about having the United States's champions kidnapped. What a laugh if the Soviet masters lost and the Americans won.

Well, Esenin would laugh loudest, because the U.S. grand master, Billy Pescador, wouldn't live to arrive at the tournament.

When Cannibal's two henchmen went back into the building, Esenin climbed out of the car and put a bug on their van.

"What did you do?" his driver asked as the KGB agent returned to the car.

"I put a homing device on the van, so we can follow it safely."

"Are they the ones we want?"

"No, but they'll lead us where we wish to go."

The young leftist squirmed, eager to get on with the game of cops and robbers.

When Lao Ti emerged from the building and accepted her car from Smith, Esenin was positive that he was on the right track. He recognized her as one of the fierce fighters who had defeated the motorcycle gang at the computer chess tournament in Monterey. Esenin had been there, disguised as a waiter.

Without turning, Esenin told his chauffeur, "Start your car. We will soon find where they have the chess players hidden."

Lao Ti arrived at the winery in time for lunch. Although she had been confident that no one knew their present whereabouts, she hadn't been without caution. She had made several detours to spot any tails she might be wearing.

Smith and Yus noticed this on the directional finder and grinned. They had never moved close enough to make visual contact with the Corvette. When it finally stopped, they approached to within several hundred yards then proceeded on foot through the vineyards.

Lao wondered whether she wouldn't have been more sensible to have had lunch on the way back. The players had agreed to remain in camp, but they had not agreed to be nice about it. Lunch was punctuated by frequent complaints and remarks about concentration camps.

Lyons threw down his fork and stalked out of the dining room, leaving most of his food uneaten. The other members of Able Team glanced at each other. It was the first time they could remember Ironman leaving while there was still food on the table.

Ignoring the negative atmosphere at the table, Politician asked Lao, "How did it go this morning?"

The members of Able Team had learned that asking Lao anything was usually a waste of time. Her answers were usually cryptic or brief to the point of nonexistence. Occasionally she was extremely informative, but the occasions were rare. Politician's question was a calculated gamble.

Lao took in the grumpy faces around the table. Then she smiled at Pol, and he allowed himself a small sigh of relief.

"Much better than I expected. I now have both the hardware and software to put together something stronger than anyone has displayed yet."

"Bullshit," Quinn snapped. "It's too soon for you to have more than promises."

"Bet me a thousand dollars?"

"You seem pretty confident," said Quinn. "I'm sorry, I left my wallet at home."

"That's too bad," said Lao.

"But we're busting with curiosity," Pescador said. "What *have* you accomplished so far?"

Lao paused before answering. "Belle now resides in my computer. This morning I picked up a larger, faster microchip to run the program. This afternoon I will mate the two."

Pescador let out a long low whistle.

"What's all that about?" Anne Harju asked.

Pescador explained, "When she gets a match, she already has something a little better than Belle, because it will think faster." He turned to Lao. "How much faster?"

"Four times."

"Does that mean it will beat you?" Harju asked.

Pescador shrugged. "It'll stand a good chance."

The Estonian stood up. "It better not. I don't intend to be a prisoner here for more than a week."

She whirled and stomped out of the room, her long blond hair swaying behind her.

IVAN ESENIN STOPPED HIS DRIVER when they were within sight of the deserted van and asked him to leave.

"I couldn't do that."

"You must. It's time for more experienced hands than mine." Esenin handed the young man a slip of paper. "Please telephone that number and tell whoever answers exactly where you left me. I'm depending on you."

When the car had disappeared, Esenin set out to watch the watchers. Twice during the afternoon, the two hardmen from Jones's team had used a shortwave radio in the van. The rest of the time, they'd munched sandwiches, swilled warm beer and watched Silklands Winery. One of them always stayed within hearing range of the radio equipment.

Esenin was still watching Cannibal's killers four hours later when the roar of motorcycles shattered the late-afternoon quiet. The KGB agent hastened up the road to meet them.

He was about half a mile up the winding road and standing in the middle of it when the motorcycles appeared. He didn't move as a 300-pound hulk on a Harley Davidson bore down on him as if determined to squash him like a bug. At the last moment, the hulk swung to one side and braked. The heavy cycle skidded to a stop with its rear wheel an inch from Esenin's toes.

"Where are they?" the hulk asked.

Esenin pointed. "Good afternoon, George. They're at Silklands Winery, which is over that hill."

"We'll squash them. Now!"

The KGB agent shook his head. "Around the next bend are two men with a van. I don't want anyone touched until those two men leave. When they do, tend to business—but do it properly this time."

"We would have done it properly before, if you'd told us about the protection. Your foul-up cost us ten of our best men." The biker's voice simmered with suppressed rage.

"I'd hardly call four bodyguards an ambush."

When he saw that his employer wasn't going to be put on the defensive, George shrugged. "No mind. They're dead meat now. There's thirty-four of us, and we're packing heavy."

Just then a horn blared, and the van went tearing past them, forcing the cyclists to scramble off the road.

"Chase that van and tear those dudes apart," the leader shouted.

Esenin shook his head.

"Cancel that," the big cyclist shouted. Then he turned to Esenin. "Those the pansies you wanted left unplucked?"

The Russian nodded.

"Then we can proceed."

"Yes, but here's a warning. The same four are still guarding them."

The biker grinned. "That will make the job a pleasure, but we'll wait until dark. I don't want to lose another man unnecessarily."

Esenin grinned. "You'll become a general yet," he told the biker.

ANNE HARJU SWEPT THE CHESSBOARD clear with her fist. "I am sick of this!"

The black man who had been quietly helping her analyze a game leaned back. He knew Harju well enough to keep his mouth shut when her temper blew.

Quinn, who was performing a similar service for Pescador, looked up and said, "It is a bloody prison here. This is worse than being in the Marines."

"It'll be interesting to see if she can get that program running, though," Pescador mused.

"Fuck the program. I want a beer."

"You were the one who wanted to bet."

"Shut up!" Quinn snapped. After a silent pause, he continued, "I vote we all go into town for a beer and some relaxation tonight."

"Think they'll let us?" asked the quiet team member, Tom Kerr.

"Who's going to ask? We'll slip out after supper, as soon as it gets dark. It'll be a nice evening for a stroll through the vines."

"I'd rather see how that program's coming," Pescador answered.

"Coach's orders, Billy. We all need a break. Don't be a spoilsport."

Pescador shrugged. "Okay." He didn't sound enthusiastic.

"It's settled then. The four chess players go for a few beers and a few laughs. The four drudges watch the empty prison."

"Is good," Harju agreed.

At that moment the four drudges were holding their own meeting on the lawn.

"We're being watched," Lyons informed the others. "They have a van parked down the road. I think we'll ask questions."

No one spoke or looked around. They waited for Lyons to disclose his plan.

"One is watching us right now from the hill behind me. The other is by the van. Gadgets and I will cut that way—" he subtly indicated a direction ahead of him "—then circle around from either side. When we're in position, Pol and Lao will start walking toward them to occupy their attention."

Each of the four habitually carried a handgun. Gadgets went inside and emerged in a few seconds with two small radios. He handed one to Pol and clipped the other on his belt.

Blancanales and Lao remained on the lawn for another twelve minutes before Pol's radio clicked twice, indicating that Gadgets and Ironman were in position. Then they rose and began walking in the prearranged direction, wondering if they were to be greeted by a hail of bullets.

As planned, Lyons and Schwarz had gone to the road and split up as Gadgets cautiously approached the van to cut off any retreat. Lyons was closing in on the man closest to the winery, and Gadgets was still a hundred yards from the van, when the side door slid open and a red-headed bean pole jumped out and ran like a rabbit into the bush.

Gadgets was tempted to study the van's communications system, but, afraid that Ironman would be sandwiched between the two unknowns, he chased the redhead.

Gadgets drew close enough to hear someone say in a stage whisper, "Quiet, Slaughter. You're making more noise than a rampaging elephant."

A gasping voice responded, "The message came. We meet them in Calistoga this evening. We can pull out and take it easy until then."

"I find the plan eminently suitable," the first voice responded in a heavy British accent.

Gadgets hid behind the bush, his silenced Beretta 93-R in hand. Out of the bush came a black man with a wild Afro surmounted by a brown cap. He made no attempt to walk quietly and moved with a trace of a limp.

"You're stoned again, O.D.," the redhead said matter-of-factly. "I'll drive."

"If that's what turns you—" the black man began, then he stumbled, cutting off the rest of his speech. But he managed to keep his balance and the two proceeded toward the van.

Gadgets looked around for Ironman. Where had he disappeared to? The question was answered as soon as it formed itself; Lyons rose from the very place where the one called O.D. had walked. Gadgets turned to intercept the two men. Lyons waved him back. They stood quietly until they heard the van roar away. Then they turned back to meet Politician and Lao.

"Why'd you let them go?" Gadgets asked.

"They already answered all my questions. We better have another planning session."

When Able Team was again assembled on the lawn outside the winery, Ironman got right down to business. "We have trouble. The Gun Team are interested in us."

Gadgets let out a low whistle.

"Who?" Lao asked.

Politician answered, "Part of a United States Army unit in Vietnam. They acquired too much of a taste for violence. And I do mean a taste. The leader, Cannibal Jones, was convicted of napalming and eating Vietnamese villagers."

"Ugh!" was Lao's gut reaction.

"Someone sprang him and four of his sidekicks after the court-martial," Lyons added. "Our files say he's doing dirty work for a few weapons manufacturers who give the entire industry a rotten name."

"Do you have a plan of attack?" Lao asked.

"Everyone get some rest," Lyons answered. "The four of us will be on guard duty tonight. They said something about meeting the rest in town, and they'll be coming here."

"We may have a rough night ahead," Lao commented.

"Count on it," Lyons said.

5

The atmosphere at supper was tense and restrained. The chess players confined their comments to asking for things to be passed; they had no intention of making a verbal slip that would give away the planned jailbreak. And the members of Able Team had reasons of their own for being quiet.

After the meal the players returned to the practice room: breaking security was one thing, but none of them would seriously consider skipping training.

Suited up in flak jackets and night camous, the Able Team fighters checked their weapons, daubed their faces and hands with black cosmetic and ventured into the twilight to take positions around the perimeter of the winery. Each carried a small communicator.

Lyons had his Konzak shotgun slung low on his back where it was least likely to snag on anything. He carried the huge silenced Python on the webbing over his flak jacket and camous, which also held a selection of grenades and magazines.

Gadgets had a silenced 93-R strapped to his left shoulder, a thin black dagger opposite. His silenced MAC-10 was in a clip on his right thigh.

Politician carried another silenced 93-R. His usual M-16/M-203 over-and-under hybrid had been left behind. It was too bulky for a stealth operation. Pol did not share Ironman's commitment to carrying an arsenal into battle. Also, the Able fighter had exchanged his white oak *jo*, or fighting stick, for a thinner one made from ironwood. The white oak stick was more properly called a *hanbo*, because it was about the length of a walking stick. The ironwood *jo* was the accepted 50-3/16 inches long but because of its strength and density was thinner than the usual 7/8 of an inch.

Lao Ti seemed minute in comparison to the three men, but she was similarly attired. A silenced Mac-11 decorated her web belt, sharing space with spare clips and *shuriken*s, the Oriental star-shaped throwing knives. Like Lyons, she depended solely on her bare hands for silent skills.

It was a cool night, and the constant patrol was tedious, but they maintained it in absolute silence. One hour had passed and the team had only starlight to guide them. The moon would not rise for another two hours.

Politician spoke into the communicators. "Lights went out in the training room. No lights have gone on in the bedrooms."

"We better check—" Lyons began.

He was interrupted by a series of clicks. Then Lao spoke in a soft but urgent tone, "A large herd of elephants, trying to walk on tiptoe, coming straight at my position."

Gadgets's voice crowded in after Lao's. "Our chess players pulling a fade from the door near the pool."

Lyons took over. "Ti, there are only five in the Gun Team. Five is not a herd."

"I guess thirty. Definitely more than twenty."

No one wasted precious seconds asking if she was sure.

"Our charges are probably headed for town," Lyons decided. "Pol, you and I will take up position south of the approaching force. Try to keep those chess idiots from blundering right into them. Gadgets, work the force from the rear. Lao, take the north side. If they get through to the buildings, it no longer matters. Their pigeons have flown the coop. Keep it quiet; we need to cut their number before they find we're here."

The four figures moved noiselessly through the vineyards to meet the approaching force.

GEORGE MARMION WAS THE NAME of the hulking leader of the Lucifers, the motorcycle gang that did Esenin's contract killing. The Lucifers called him Mar; most of them did not know his real name. For such a large man, he moved lightly on his feet.

As he led his heavily armed band through the vineyards, he was proud of their discipline. Vietnam had taught Mar the importance of good training. He was able to force the training on his troops because the money from drugs and contract killings made the Lucifers a choice gang. He had been able to assemble thirty-four experienced killers for this wipeout.

Mar thought his troops moved well through the vineyards. Pimples, as one Lucifer was nicknamed, had tripped on something and fallen heavily; he'd have to run the gauntlet later for his clumsiness. But on the whole his boys were moving as well as Mar's unit had moved in the Vietnamese jungles. It helped that any man who broke silence would be docked a week's pay.

At the edge of the Silklands vineyard, he looked across the cleared area to the winery buildings. So far, there had been no sign of the deadly bodyguards. There were few lights on in the building. Mar concluded that the pampered little chess players had been tucked in early. He waved for his men to spread out along the edge of the vineyard before moving across the open area.

Mar noticed his gang members were improving with practice. They were less noisy now than when they'd started out.

LAO TI'S MAIN MARTIAL SKILL was *aikido*, the Japanese martial art that turns force back on itself. As she heard the still-distant army approach, she could hear the voice of Sensei Kemuri, the master who had instructed her from her third birthday until she had left Japan at the age of twenty-two to study for her degree. She perpetually heard his wisdom in the silence of her heart.

She had been twelve when he called her to him after practice to tell her, "You progress well, Little Mixingpot." He called her that because of her mixed Vietnamese and Mongolian heritage. "Now, you must journey into other disciplines.

"You were begun on your path at a choice age. Already you need fear an attack from no one. From now on, you must blend in other arts and learn to attack effectively."

The idea of learning to attack had shocked Lao as nothing else could have. Kemuri had watched over the development of the girl's mind with even more care than he did over the development of her body. He approved of her involvement in computers. Her father, an American-trained Mongolian computer scientist, had always had a computer in the home. Kemuri had added a stark perception of sexuality, brutality and depravity to the young girl's awareness. To the master, a human who could be shocked was not safe, not self-reliant.

Once he deigned to explain, "I know that all your *aikido* training had ingrained in you the belief that you must wait for the other to attack and then turn the attacker's force back on himself. This is a good principle for both the martial arts and for living your life. But there is an exception. We must now train you for the exception.

"I have taken pains to point out to you that this is not a just world. Justice is a virtue to be striven for, never a perpetual state. You can now care for yourself, but if you cannot attack you cannot care for others. Sometimes, to preserve the purity of your own heart, you must strike the first blow."

She had not understood at the time. Her Taoist and *aikido* training had penetrated too deeply. But over the next ten years, Kemuri had not been her only instructor. There was always a sensei from another discipline to aid in her teaching. Always the process included much discussion and thinking, so the process integrated the other arts into the *aikido* and did not conflict with it.

Since she had joined the Stony Man group, Lao had understood. She eyed the army coming toward her, knowing that they would die and that she would initiate the action.

Upon instructions from Lyons, Lao advanced quietly to her right, searching for flankers. There were none. The enemy moved forward in a single column, sacrificing safe procedure to keep the troops from going astray. It would be difficult to thin their ranks without alerting the entire group.

A splashing sound attracted her attention: a gang member with an M-203 slung over his shoulder had stepped to the side of the column to urinate.

Lao chopped down on his bent spine with an open axhand, crushing his fifth cervical vertebra. The broken bone shards were driven into the spinal nerves, severing communications with the lower body. The dead man fell forward into his own puddle.

Lao stepped back as two forms detached themselves from the column to investigate the noise made by the falling corpse.

Oblivious of the shadowy form standing two paces away, the city-trained goons bent over the fallen member of their pack. One received a small fist with the middle knuckle extended into his temple; he folded over the other corpse.

The other killer was standing straight. The fingers of Lao's right hand went rigid, forming a U with the thumb. They drove forward into the killer's throat with the relentless power of a masonry nail fired from a gun.

The U clamped around his larynx and tightened. A quarter-century of *aikido* training made her small hands an effective vice. The goon kicked a few times, unable even to shout, then died from shock.

Lao glanced back at the column. One man had stopped and was standing to one side, staring at her.

GADGETS SCHWARZ FOUND THE END of the column quickly. He simply glided over the soft earth in the opposite direction to the column, keeping a row of vines between himself and the intruders. He then stepped behind the column and listened. Hearing no one else approaching, he ran silently on his toes until he was behind the trail man.

Schwarz reached across his web belt and removed his dagger from the sheath over his right shoulder.

The trailing man had an old Thompson slung over his right shoulder. Gadgets's right arm snaked around the big subgun, his hand covering the thug's mouth, his thumb pinching the nose shut against his index finger. With his left arm, he plunged the dagger into the man's heart.

Gadget's held the man until there was no more movement, then lowered the corpse to the ground. Retrieving his thin-bladed knife, he took off after the line to eliminate the next man.

The character in front of Gadgets wore a motorcycle jacket and carried a pump shotgun diagonally across the chest, making a repeat of Gadgets's last maneuver impractical. The Able Team warrior shifted the dagger to his right hand and trapped the thug's mouth and nose with his left. His right hand rammed the blade home, slicing through the kidney. The goon died instantly, silently.

As Gadgets lowered the body to the ground, a voice from the back of the column growled, "What the hell's going on back there?"

LYONS AND POLITICIAN didn't like their position, but the chess players who were sneaking into town gave them no choice. Without a force between the two groups, they were bound to stumble into each other, with potentially disastrous results.

To make things worse, the players were making no effort to move silently. They believed that Able Team, supposedly back at the winery, was the only reason for caution. Fortunately the cultivated ground muffled their footfalls, and they kept their voices low in case an Able Team member was lurking on the grounds.

"Boy, am I looking forward to a cold beer!" Quinn said, a bit too loudly and enthusiastically.

Immediately two heads snapped around in the line of heavily armed thugs. Lyons saw one man tap the shoulders of two others and lead them toward the voice they had heard.

Lyons stepped back slowly, hiding amidst the vines. Politician likewise transformed himself into a shapeless mass in the dark. When the first gang member came within striking range, the *jo* sung a low note, ending with a distinct crack as it connected with a shin.

Letting out a muffled cry, the gang member dropped his hunting rifle and rolled along the ground, hugging his shin. The other two veered to their fallen brother-in-gore.

"What happened?" one whispered, kneeling.

"Barked my shin," the fallen one gasped.

"Is that all? Get up."

Lyons stepped behind the one who was still standing and kicked the base of his skull. In karate practice Lyons could break three-inch-thick pine boards with either of his legs. Applied to the subhuman before him now, the force of his kick stretched the man's neck and snapped the spine. The human football never knew that he pitched straight onto his face. He was dead before he felt the kick.

Pol took care of the other two. From his crouched position, he thrust with the *jo* like a fencer making a lunge. The tip of the stick struck one of the bikers just behind the ear where the skull plates join. The kneeling man fell, kicked once and died. Only the goon with the damaged shin remained. But before he could yell, a thin bar closed down on his exposed neck. Over him loomed a large man, putting his full weight on the stick. It crushed his windpipe and closed off the arteries. The goon's boots dug two troughs in the soft soil before he followed his dead brethren into hell.

Lyons had already moved on to warn the chess players how near they were to danger.

6

As he sped to catch up with the chess players, Lyons thought of Lao, who had an entire flank to control. Could the small silent woman handle such a large area and so many enemy troops?

And who was the enemy? Able Team was guarding the American chess team, true, but their main objective had been to help two Russians escape to the West. Now it seemed as though the major problem was keeping the Americans alive. Who was trying to kill them, and why?

Lyons caught sight of Anne Harju's long blond hair, swinging in the starlight. He also caught sight of four silent forms closing in on her for a surprise attack.

Sprinting to take out the killers before they could kill the chess players, Lyons caught the glint of a knife blade.

Quinn, unaware of danger, chuckled and said, "Those four suckers are back there guarding an empty hen coop. What a laugh!"

At that moment Lyons grabbed the back of a gang member's neck with one hand while the other cupped the chin. Lyons gave a sudden wrench; the neck broke and he dropped the corpse and rushed the next attacker.

The first kill had not been silent. The sound of the breaking neck was distinct against the background songs of frogs and insects. The other three attackers also heard the soft plop when the body hit the ground. They spun to face Lyons, even as he dived at one of them.

Lyons's intended victim saw him coming. That was all he ever saw. With his right fist Lyons snapped a two-knuckle blow to the larynx. The punch was as deadly as a .45 bullet.

The two others, unaware they faced a killing machine, spread out, determined to eliminate him. They came at him from opposite sides, holding knives low, ready to slash or thrust.

Lyons's right leg shot out to an arm and knife. The heel of his combat boot pulverized the sternum, driving slivers of bone into the lungs and heart. The corpse was thrown into a tangle of grapevines.

Lyons's foot lashed out sideways as he leaned to the left and grabbed the wrist of the final attacker's knife hand. As Lyons lowered his right leg, he straightened, dragging the knife wielder toward him and delivering a powerful punch to the gang member's soft belly.

Air whooshed from the killer's lungs, and he doubled over in short-lived agony. Lyons swung his left fist to the temple and kicked the man in the neck as the body fell. The neck snapped.

Lyons took a deep breath and looked around. The chess players were out of sight. So was the line of heavily armed motorcycle troops. But at least one remained nearby, for Lyons heard a voice saying "What the hell's going on back there?"

The ex-LAPD member moved silently through the vines for a better view in the starlight. The man who had spoken was looking away from Lyons. His question had brought three others.

Lyons's brow furrowed. How were he and Gadgets going to silence these four before they alerted the entire troop? At least one of the motorcyclists was certain to shout before either Gadgets or Lyons could close the distance.

FIFTEEN FEET FROM THE SINGLE FILE of hoodlums who were closing in on Silklands Winery, Lao saw one of them staring at her: she had the sinking feeling she had given the game away. As he moved a single step closer, Lao realized he could see the nonblackened hands and faces of the three dead goons, but not her. Kemuri's voice sounded deep within her, as it often did in times of stress. *"A swordsman knows his mind and weapon are one. This is especially true for you, because your body is your weapon. Never ask yourself 'What do I do now?' Empty your mind and let your weapon do what it has been trained to do."*

Instead of worrying about the man who had just taken another step closer, Lao blanked her mind, leaving her body and will to choose the appropriate action.

With her blackened hand she grabbed the wrist of the man she had just killed and moved it in a low circular motion, so that it seemed to beckon the onlooker closer.

He stepped forward, mumbling, "What is it?"

The hand waved once more then dropped. Curiosity overcame caution, and the man approached. Behind him, his fellow goons continued to move toward the target zone.

Lao drew herself into a ball, balanced on her toes. When the onlooker was eight feet away, she sprang, snapping her arms forward. Her arms thrusting ahead of her, fingers rigid, Lao was a human spear. With the force of 120 hurtling pounds behind them as they reached the solar plexus, her hands pierced the skin, mashed intestines and snapped the spine. Before Lao retracted her hands, the curious one was searching hell for his guts.

Lao gave the astonished motorcyclists no chance to recover from the shadowy sight of one of their number being torn apart by a small, slight form. Those who had seen the action froze in their tracks. Springing into action, she started throwing punches.

A CLUMP OF GRAPEVINE brushing his back, Politician stood silently in the moonless night, a mottled gray blob against a mottled gray background. Four feet away a ragtag assortment of killers, each heavily armed, passed in single file.

Politician thrust with his *jo*, the way a fencer thrusts. The tip of the deadly stick caught a head on the temple, cracking the skull, killing instantly. The gang member toppled sideways, away from Pol.

The next in line stopped immediately.

"What's wrong?" someone else whispered.

"Max just collapsed. Help me get him up."

As the two went to help, the one next in line detoured to catch up with the others. His detour took him close to Pol. A whistling *jo* crushed the thug's windpipe. He collapsed, gargling his own blood.

The two who were trying to help Max were Pol's next targets. He jabbed down hard on a bent back, mashing the exposed kidney. The target gasped then collapsed on the other punk who had been kneeling.

"What's happening?" someone demanded in a voice that shook with terror.

"Someone's in that bush." Pointing to the vines where Pol stood, he raised his rifle.

LYONS DECIDED that the fun was over. The advantage of surprise had to be exchanged for the power of artillery. Crouching, he slid the silenced Python from its leather and aligned with a head silhouetted against the stars. The eight-inch barrel plus the custom suppressor and laser beam night sight made it a heavy weapon. But Ironman's karate-trained wrists held the sight level and steady.

The Colt gave a sharp cough. The compression effect of the .45 bullet tore into the motorcyclist's head, splattering a nearby gang member.

The second man let out a scream of terror. He was next to die as Lyons sent a .45 into his temple. As the gang member's scream echoed through the night, Gadgets readied his 93-R, which wasn't equipped with a laser sight. Two goons were running toward him with their weapons leveled. Lining up on one of them, he squeezed off his first shot and tracked to the second target, who had turned toward the sound of Ironman's Python. Gadgets had scored one clear head shot after another.

Those who had paused were now out of the way, and Lyons and Gadgets moved toward the other gang members, whom they knew to be fully alerted to their presence and ready for combat.

LAO'S DARK FORM MATERIALIZED like the angel of death in front of five of the killers. With the middle knuckle of her right hand sticking out of her fist, she launched a straight jab at the first.

Thudding into the target's solar plexus, the small hard fist traumatized the vagus nerve, stopping all impulses to the diaphragm. The killer dropped in agony, his lungs unable to draw air.

The 250-pound ape on the dying man's left had time to say "Hell! It's only a girl."

Lao's foot moved faster than the eye could follow and smashed into the ape's testicles. He managed only a high-pitched moan as he fainted.

The three others silently and unanimously decided that they needed more space between themselves and the girl. Stepping back, they brought their weapons to bear. But two of them backed into the fatal embraces of Gadgets and Ironman, who had just arrived on the scene.

Gadgets holstered his gun with one hand as he drew the dagger with the other. He wrapped his arm around one gang member and plunged the blade into his kidney. A twist of the blade brought such agony that the man's face contorted into a silent scream. He collapsed, dead of trauma before he hit the ground.

As Lyons collided with one figure, another appeared on his right. Lyons wrapped his left arm around the man in front of him, then raised his Colt Python and fired. The bullet traveled three inches to replace the killer's evil thoughts—a real mindblower.

The third retreating killer had enough presence of mind to fire his weapon. But since Lao had enough presence of mind to have swerved, the bullet whizzed by only inches from her head. She lunged at her target and snaked her arm around his neck. With a quick twist, she snapped the man's neck.

Lyons and Gadgets and Lao looked at one another over the littered battlefield. No one said anything. Lyons freshened the Colt's cylinder. Lao slowly drew her silenced Mac-11. Then the three warriors took off after the invaders once more.

EVEN AS THE KILLER was raising his rifle, Pol was cautiously shifting position. But instead of moving away from the gang members, he moved toward them, hoping to blend into the group without anyone taking too much notice.

"No one's in there," Pol said in a gruff voice.

Someone made a tentative kick at the vines and then waded in. The other three waited.

"No one here," said the one exploring the vines.

Pol moved closer: not close enough that anyone could make him out by starlight, but close enough to be considered part of the group, instead of a threat.

"What's happening? Who's firing on us?" another asked, his voice quavering.

Pol heard footsteps and knew that three Able Team warriors were closing in. He delivered a stunning blow from the *jo* to the head of the nearest man. Then he kicked the head of another hood and continued with the same sweeping motion to break the gun wrist of another.

Then Lyons's Python coughed, and a hoodlum's brain became mush. Three others fell a moment later, victims of the superb combat training of Lao, Gadgets and Pol.

United again, the four moved to the remaining group of Lucifers, guided by the voice of the gang leader, George Marmion, who barked, "Come on, guys, spread out."

Just then Mar saw the four materialize out of the darkness. Funny, he didn't remember any of his men being as small as the smallest of this lot.

"What's keeping you?" he demanded in a hoarse whisper.

"You are, but not for long," said the coldest voice Mar had ever heard.

It was also the last voice he ever heard. Four silenced guns fired. The remaining Lucifers left for their class reunion in hell.

"That's the last of 'em," said Pol. "That was the most disorganized army of thugs it's ever been my pleasure to eliminate."

Lao took a deep breath. "The next ones may be more organized. Whoever's after our chess team obviously wants them out of the way pretty badly."

"Speaking of the chess players, where are they?" asked Lyons.

"Seems like they snuck out on us," said Gadgets. "Last I saw of 'em they were heading for town."

"Well, we'd better get the grease and fatigues off," Lyons said. "Let's get to town before those chess players find more trouble."

7

The three-mile hike to town was pleasant for the four players who were enjoying a thrill similar to the type felt by children playing hooky.

The town, famous for is hot spring mud baths, was quiet in the pretourist season. On the main street, which, due to the absence of high buildings, seemed wider that it actually was, Quinn called to an elderly resident with a ramrod straight back, "Hey, old-timer, where does a thirsty traveler find an honest beer?"

The man glared at the blond young man. "There's no such thing," he answered. "People without taste generally drink at the International, two blocks further on."

He strode off, leaving the chess coach glowering at his erect back and the others laughing.

"Come on," Pescador said. "It sounds like he was describing exactly the sort of place you need."

Quinn followed the rest of them down the street and into the shoddiest looking building in town.

The four truants went to the stand-up bar because the six tables were occupied. It took no great detective to see that the customers were divided into two distinct camps, an older group of regulars and about a dozen toughs who were shooting snooker at the two pool tables. The chess players ordered beers then turned to casually study the pool players.

In addition to the group of tough-looking dudes around the tables, another four watched, making conversation and heavy side-bets.

Two of them were especially interesting: one was a short sandy-haired man with a prominent Adam's apple and an Irish accent; the other was bald, light-skinned, militarily erect, an older man who seemed to be giving the first a briefing. Shaughnessy O'Hearn, the mercenary, listened carefully as Cannibal Jones described each of the four members of the American chess team in detail.

"I wonder what those two are plotting," Quinn said.

Pescador was watching a table where $200 in bets rode on the next shot. Without turning, he said, "Probably whether to have you fried or raw for breakfast. Finish your beer so we can go somewhere else."

Quinn said, "I like it here. Real people."

"Maybe you think we were manufactured in a plastic factory," Harju snapped. "Do not even bother to finish your beer. We are leaving now."

One of only two women in the place, Harju was receiving more than her share of attention, but none of it was making her feel like a human being. The other woman had short golden hair, translucent green eyes and a glowing complexion. She was with the toughs at the pool tables and didn't seem to mind the lecherous stares.

Harju slid off the bar stool and turned toward the door. Quinn grabbed her wrist and yanked her back.

"Sit down and finish your beer."

One of the pool players had been eyeing Harju since she had arrived. He was a tall red-headed bean pole, wearing cowboy boots, jeans and a fancy shirt. When he saw Quinn grab Harju, he was at her side in a flash.

"I'll be glad to take care of this punk, little lady."

Anne knew in her gut that a large dose of trouble had arrived. She tried to use reason to stave off disaster.

"He does not mean anything. . . ."

"You heard the woman," Quinn interrupted. "Fuck off."

The words worked like a magician's incantation. For a moment the atmosphere was taut with hushed expectancy. The pool players became silent, glancing at the three main actors. The regulars at the tables froze.

Over the sudden quiet Shaughnessy O'Hearn addressed the bald man in his distinctive Irish brogue, "What were those descriptions again?" He gestured toward the four chess players.

Jones opened his mouth in disbelief then said, "You're right. Take care of them."

The redheaded cowboy seemed to gain bravado from the suddenly quiet room. A slow grin spread over his freckled face. Then he whipped up the butt of his pool cue and bestowed upon Quinn a glancing blow to the jaw.

"That's no way to talk in front of a lady," he said. This rhinestone cowboy, a member of the Gun Team, sported no trace of a Western accent. His name was Slaughter Smith, and for good reason. His speech sounded more like the grunts of a primitive man.

Quinn splashed his beer into his attacker's face as the tip of the cue was coming around again. It smashed into Quinn's wrist, causing the glass to fly from his hand.

Sliding off the stool, Quinn planted a short right in his tormentor's gut, knocking him back but not slowing him down.

"You're not being friendly," Smith grunted. As he raised the cue again, Cannibal Jones placed a restraining hand on his shoulder.

"Take a good look," Jones told the fighting cowboy. "These people belong to our friends."

Smith's jaw dropped. He scrutinized Harju, Pescador, Quinn and Tom Kerr—the young visitor who'd been helping Harju train. Then his face regained its grin of animal delight.

"This one's not in the deal, Cannibal. I can have him."

"You're right," said Cannibal Jones.

"What's going on?" Harju demanded. No one answered her.

The members of the Gun Team and most of the pool players began to gather around. Deciding it was time to get reinforcements, Pescador and Kerr bolted for the door.

In a calm voice Jones ordered, "Don't let those two get away."

Blocking the door, a six-foot-six hulk shoved Pescador back into the hands of half a dozen thugs. "Don't hurt that one!" Jones ordered. Then the hulk—Feces Fatheringham—wrapped one huge paw around Kerr's head. He picked up the young chess player as easily as if there were no body attached to the head. He swung him around until he felt and heard the neck snap then threw the corpse in a corner.

Pescador had no chance. He was raised bodily from the floor by a huge thug and carried out the door. Someone else followed, keeping a strong hand clasped over his mouth.

Two men grabbed Anne Harju's arms; another shoved a fistful of paper napkins into her mouth. Then she was hustled out the door, her feet dragging on the floor. She took a last glance back and wished she hadn't.

Slaughter Smith renewed his attack on Quinn, who was now simply a witness to be eliminated. This time, when he swung his pool cue, he caught the chess coach between the legs.

As Quinn doubled over, Smith grabbed his short blond hair and yanked, propelling Quinn across the room. Smith followed, slamming the butt of the stick into the base of Quinn's spine. Screaming, Quinn collapsed.

The rest of Quinn's life was not sweet. Whenever he stirred, the butt of the cue slammed into him. He grabbed at a combat boot and had his elbow smashed. He curled into a fetal position, and the whistling pool stick smashed two of his ribs. He tried lying still, and a combat boot kicked him between the legs. His one piece of luck: he died one-third of the way through the vicious beating.

It took Able Team only five minutes to strip out of their battle fatigues, remove the black warpaint from their faces and hands, get dressed and don their weapons in concealed leather. Two minutes later they were speeding to Calistoga in Pol's van. They arrived in time to see a tough-looking gang toss Pescador and Harju into the canvas-topped back of a two-ton four-by-four truck. About ten men, ranging in age from twenty to forty, piled in with their prisoners.

Seeing the truck take off, Politician stepped on the gas. The two vehicles rolled through town at over sixty miles per hour, forcing all other cars on the road to the curb.

"They've got Harju and Pescador in there," said Lao, "but what's happened to Tom Kerr and Upton Quinn?"

"Either dead or escaped," said Ironman. "We'll know soon enough."

They were clearing town when Gadgets said, "Another van on our tail. Looks like the one that was hanging around Silklands earlier today."

Lyons seldom vented frustration verbally, but this time he let out several choice curse words. They were directed at himself for advising the team to carry only hand weapons. He had thought they were simply going to scoop the four chess players as quietly as possible.

"The van in back is gaining quickly," Politician observed, glancing in the rearview mirror, "and I've got this baby wide open."

Lyon's pulled out his Python and removed the suppressor: he needed all the punch he could get. Ahead, the truck weaved to keep the Able Team vehicle from coming alongside. Because of the weaving, the men in the back didn't try to shoot. But Able Team could do nothing to stop the truck without endangering the chess players.

The van behind them was soon overtaking them, its supercharger whining like a banshee. Gadgets pulled his Mac-10 from under his sport jacket and used it to hammer out a rear window.

"My van!" Pol protested.

"Our asses! Some woman is lining up a tiny subgun on us from the passenger side."

Gadgets forgot whatever else he was going to say. He threw himself flat as a stream of bullets ate away a corner of the van's roof.

"What shoots like that?" Lao wondered.

No one answered as Politician started to swerve the van. Gadgets held on to the seat, firing short bursts across the windshield of the chase vehicle.

"Bulletproof glass," he reported, "but at least now they're having trouble seeing."

"Get off the road," Lyons ordered.

"The chess players—" Pol began.

"Now!"

Pol yelled, "Hold on!" and steered the van toward a ditch on the right.

The ditch was steep, and only Politician's superior driving skill kept the vehicle from rolling over.

"Through that field," Lyons commanded, indicating a field of spring wheat less than five inches high.

"Too soft."

"As far as you can go."

While Politican sweated at the wheel, Lyons shouted instructions. "Split up. Don't engage the enemy unless cornered. Meet back in town at the first church on this side of town.''

Lyons seldom ordered Able Team to flee; never before had it been every man for himself. Yet such was the team's faith in his snap decisions that no one asked questions. Each simply followed orders.

Politician skillfully maneuvered the van a quarter-mile into the field. He hadn't tried to maintain speed; instead, he had given the van as much gas as he could without over-revving it and needlessly spinning the wheels. As a result, the wheels did not dig themselves into deep trenches.

The moment the van stopped, everyone bailed out. Behind them, as they quickly noticed, the other van had bogged down within fifteen feet of crossing the ditch; it was armored, therefore heavier, and the driver had been a shade less skillful than Pol. This gave Able Team a brief head start. They needed it. Bullets whizzed by only slightly short of their position.

Silently they split up and ran for the trees at the edge of the field. No one bothered trying to zigzag: it was more important to keep their advantage of distance. Politician got hit twice, but his body armor absorbed the impact. The others safely reached the tree-lined fence rows at different places and went to ground. Pol made it, too, but he knew he'd be sporting some beautiful bruises for a few weeks.

At the edge of the field, they looked back. To their relief, Cannibal Jones's team was in retreat.

Able Team watched the Gun Team use their communications gear—possibly to call for a tow truck—then search and torch Politician's van. After the enemy left, Able Team returned one by one to town.

"Why did we let them go?" Lao asked when they were reassembled in a churchyard in Calistoga.

Ironman gave her a frosty stare. There was a prolonged silence as he debated with himself whether he should answer.

"The lot of you start spending more time in the rec room," Lyons ordered.

The "rec room" meant the Stony Man recognition center where files on terrorists and other important criminals were constantly updated. Lyons spent much of his free time there; Politician and Gadgets spent some off-duty time there, but when they weren't on assignment, they usually left Stony Man to tend to their private lives.

Lyons gave them a condensed briefing. "Colonel Caruthers Jones—alias Cannibal—and the four members of his team were convicted of atrocities in Vietnam. They were a crack fighting unit. Someone sprang them from military prison before they could be shot. They do the occasional free-lance job and regularly do the muscle work for a few dirty arms makers. The arms makers equip them with the best, much of it prototypes not available to others.

"They have enough firepower to blast us in to the outer stratosphere. You saw what the AM180 did to the van."

"It shoots .22s, doesn't it?" Lao asked.

"Yeah. It shoots common .22 longs, but it zips them so fast the AM180 has more punch than a .45 auto. The thing shoots through cinder block and sheet steel."

"Too much."

"That's just their light stuff," Lyons continued. "They've got heavy stuff that can do real damage."

"Why'd they back off?" Gadgets asked.

"Cannibal Jones is crazy, not stupid. He doesn't take unnecessary risks. If he can achieve the objective without loss, he will."

"His men are more like a company than a team," Pol said. "I counted about ten in the back of the truck and five more in the van."

"He hired mercenaries to do the snatch. That was Gun Team in the van."

"How do you know?"

"I read the damn files! Gun Team is five. They hired Shaughnessy O'Hearn; I recognized him getting into that truck. His crew usually totals twelve. They're no problem. Just the usual mercenaries."

"How do you know?" Pol asked again.

"I read the damn files."

When the team had run out of questions, Lyons began laying out a course of action.

"Pol, get on to Stony Man. Have them put us together transportation at least as good as the van that took us out today. Make sure it has smuggler's caches for our weapons. Tell them two days; settle for three.

"Ti, get that fancy computer of yours off playing games. Find out why in hell the Gun Team wants our chess players.

"Gadgets, rent us a temporary vehicle. Make damn sure Silklands isn't being watched then pull our stuff out. Set Ti up with her computer someplace then come and get me."

"Where will you be?"

"Finding out what went down here."

"They'll be watching the International."

"I'll take care of that first. It'll be my job to see whether Quinn and Kerr are dead or alive. Why are you three still hanging around? If we want Harju and Pescador back alive, we'll have to hustle."

8

O'Hearn and his terrorist mercenaries were staying at their usual Los Angeles hotel, Lyons figured. He had little doubt that O'Hearn checked with the hotel for messages each day—a mercenary cannot afford to forget his mail. The problem was that O'Hearn wasn't so stupid that he'd let his message service know his whereabouts. Able Team decided to drop O'Hearn a note.

The problem with using telephone messages to track someone down is that the tracker is left without a trail. Wanting O'Hearn to pick up the message in person, Lyons left an envelope at the hotel containing the halves of five one-thousand-dollar bills. The bait was irresistible to a mercenary—money plus mystery.

Lyons, Schwarz, Blancanales and Lao arrived at the hotel an hour before the envelope was delivered. They drove up in what appeared to be a large Magic Wagon. Actually, the factory had rushed it through under the direction of Stony Man engineers, putting a huge engine in an armored body while preserving the appearance of an assembly-line product. The job had been completed in three days.

After the messenger service brought the envelope for O'Hearn, Lao remained stationed in the lobby. Luckily O'Hearn called in after only a couple of hours. Lao saw the desk clerk put down the telephone, slit open the envelope then report back to the person on the other end.

Able Team was set for action when O'Hearn appeared shortly after nine o'clock. Twenty seconds after the merc left his car, Gadgets had planted a bug on it. As O'Hearn approached the desk, Lao bumped into him and planted another miniature transmitter under his jacket collar. These were a new, miniaturized specialty that Gadgets had cooked up with Lao's help. They could transmit any sound within ten feet or a tracking signal.

After a quick drink at the bar, O'Hearn was on his way. Able Team followed in two vehicles. Lao drove a rented Corvette with Ironman riding shotgun. Politician drove the van, which he had already christened the "Able wagon"; Gadgets sat in the back, monitoring the electronics gear.

SMITH FLICKED HIS COMMUNICATOR to Send and told Cannibal, "O'Hearn's returning."

"O.D. checking to see he's clean?"

"Yeah, man, but where would he pick up a bug?"

"Just check."

Cannibal Jones had not survived years of being hunted by military police, military intelligence, the FBI and the secret services of half a dozen other nations by placing blind trust in mercenary hirelings. He had hired O'Hearn and his group then concentrated on monitoring their every movement. He didn't trust O'Hearn not to pull a double-cross or a blunder.

The Gun Team expected Able Team to come after the prisoners as any mercenary who flubbed a bodyguard job would do. Their first encounter with Able Team had raised Cannibal's respect for the unknown bodyguards, but not his fear of them. Any sensible soldier knows when to retreat, but the ability to run didn't mean they couldn't fight.

O'Hearn's group had taken the two captives to a group of fifteen tourist cabins that weren't scheduled to open for another month. They rented them from the old couple who managed the camp, which had been chosen because the prisoners could be kept in virtual isolation.

By the next day, O.D. installed a fancy wire fence along the road to the camp. Actually it was a two-hundred-yard antenna. Smith's electronic monitoring gear sniffed everything that went past for broadcast units and bugs. It was this fence that now told O.D. that O'Hearn was wearing a bug.

"Shit!" Jones's voice squawked on the communicator. "Whoever those birds are, they're sharper than I thought. They'll probably attack tonight. Get the crew together. We want to be in position to sandwich the bastards between ourselves and O'Hearn's boys."

9

"I'm getting the spy satellite blowups now," Lao told the Able Team warriors.

They gathered around her computer screen as her fingers danced over the keys, producing a larger image of the tourist cabins.

"Looks like they've kept to the cabins nearest the road," Politician remarked.

"I don't think so. Look at this." Lao punched some more keys. The scene changed color.

"What's this?"

"The same thing in infrared. See those spots at the far end?"

"They've left their vehicles and a couple of guards at one end. Most of the people are at the other. Is that it?" Lyons demanded.

Lao nodded.

"Where's the van that almost cashed in our chips four days ago?"

"Too many of that kind of vehicle around. I can't identify it on my screen."

Lyons stared at the monitor.

"Let's go," he snapped.

"Now?" Gadgets asked. "Why not wait for dark?"

"That's what the Gun Team expects us to do."

Thirty minutes later Politician pulled the van into the drive leading to the tourist cabins; Lao was beside him,

Lyons and Schwarz were in the back. The team was outfitted for war.

CANNIBAL JONES AND HIS TEAM assembled a quarter of a mile up the mountain from the tourist cabins. They had an excellent view of the approach to the cabins. He kept his binoculars trained on the road.

"Van approaching," he told the four other members of his team. "Hard to see who's in it. One of O'Hearn's wimps is waving it down. It's slowing; looks like they're going to try to bluff their way in. Let's get moving."

The Gun Team jogged toward the road. Puffing hard, Jones said, "They're going to be fighting it out. We can move in and take care of any who survive."

"As long as we get to annihilate someone," Slaughter Smith commented.

At the checkpoint Politician rolled down his window as he slowed down by the mercenary guard. When the man bent to look into the van, Politician delivered a short hard two-knuckle blow to his eyes. As the guard staggered away, pressing his palms to his eyes, Pol floored the accelerator. Able Team reached the last two cabins without alerting O'Hearn's elite kidnappers.

"Take the front!" Lyons yelled at Lao. "You two take the end cabin," he commanded Gadgets and Pol.

Holding the Konzak cradled across his chest, Ironman took four huge strides then leaped through the rear window of the closest cabin. He straightened slightly then tucked and rolled when his boots hit the floor. He was in a small kitchen.

A voice from the front room said, "What the hell?"

Lyons appeared at the door to the cabin's main room as Lao kicked open the front door. Two of the kidnappers had drawn weapons and had grabbed the hostages. A third was crouched between two beds, training a .44 Magnum revolver at Lyons's chest.

Lao's Mac-11 spoke first; an automatic burst of four .380 ACPs tore two-thirds of the crouching kidnapper's neck away. He slowly collapsed, spraying a bed with blood.

"Throw down your weapons or the prisoners get wiped!" a short man shouted. He held a Colt 1911 to Pescador's head.

GADGETS TOOK THE FRONT DOOR of the end cabin, Politician the back window. As Pol raced around the clapboard structure, he saw movement inside the kitchen at the rear. Pol's M-203 belched immediately, smashing a tear gas grenade through the kitchen window.

Someone yelled "What the hell!" then was consumed by a fit of coughing.

Politician yanked up a gas mask from around his neck, reloaded the M-203, kicked the lower sash out of the window frame and stepped inside. Whoever had been in the kitchen had retreated to the main room of the cabin, shutting the door between the two rooms.

Politician picked up a pot and hurled it at the door. The moment it struck, six bullets perforated the door panels.

Pol stealthily stepped outside again and fired his HE grenade into the kitchen wall. He snapped in a tear gas grenade and waited for the smoke and dust to clear. As soon as he could see the hole the High Explosive grenade had punched through the wall, Pol fired the tear gas canister through the hole into the front room.

Gadgets waited until he heard firing from inside the cabin. The five mercenaries inside had evidently been playing cards. Four were now firing at the rear of the cabin while one watched the front.

Gadgets pulled a tear gas grenade from his web belt. He smashed his fist through the glass and dropped the grenade. The mercenaries whirled to the side window, firing as they spun. Just then an explosion blasted a hole in the rear wall. The kidnappers threw themselves flat as Pol's tear gas grenade bounced off the ceiling and burst in their midst.

Gadgets pulled his mask into place as he ran for the front door. He stood flat against the wall and waited.

Pol climbed into the kitchen again, kicked open the door to the main room and jumped back. Two bullets penetrated the doorjamb. He looked to see the occupants by the front door, readying to burst out.

Pol crossed the room and swung the butt of the M-16/ M-203 combo at the back of the first head he encountered. Then Gadgets struck, slamming his fists simultaneously into the necks of two mercs, who had rushed outside, causing immediate unconsciousness. He leaped off the small front porch at the two remaining mercenaries who were spinning around, rubbing their stinging eyes.

Before they were sure which way their guns were pointing, Schwarz was between them. As his right elbow snapped into a crotch, making one man double over with a loud wail, his left fist hammered the other's thigh muscle, throwing him off balance. Then Gadgets's right fist smashed into the gun wrist. A bone snapped, and an automatic dropped to the ground.

The vanquished men were securely bound with handcuffs. The two Able Team warriors were ready to go and see how Lyons and Ti were managing when a burst of automatic fire crackled just over their heads. They hit the ground.

"Looks like we get to meet the Gun Team again," Pol commented, trying to ascertain the source of the bullets.

BEFORE EITHER LYONS OR LAO could react to the demand to throw down their weapons, the two chess players raised their arms, let their knees buckle, and as if in tandem, slid below the guns being held against their heads. It took the kidnappers half a second to adjust—half a second too long.

Lao had a clear shot of the goon who had been holding Pescador. The moment he slid down, she triggered a short burst that scalped the goon, splattering his brain.

Holding the Konzak in his hands, Lyons couldn't fire at the other goon without hitting Harju. Instead he lunged with the assault shotgun aimed forward as if he were making a rapier thrust, crossed the room in a couple of strides and forced the barrel of the Konzak into the kidnapper's eye.

The man screamed and jerked back, releasing Harju, who immediately rolled to one side. Lyons straightened and brought the Konzak back to where he could make it speak. The assault shotgun barked once, blowing the kidnapper's head off.

"Come on," Lyons said. "Move fast."

First each of the chess players picked up an automatic that had been dropped by the kidnappers then they followed Lyons through the back window. Lao brought up the rear.

Lyons moved cautiously to the corner of the building and peered around carefully. Automatic weapon fire burst out from two directions. Closing in along Able Team's back track, O'Hearn and several men fired at someone in front of the cabins. The other fusillade came from uphill, beyond the last cabin. Gadgets and Pol were boxed in.

"Get those two to the van," Lyons barked at Lao, knowing that her weapon's range was too short for this type of fight, anyhow.

Lao looked around then led her charges in a circular route that would give them the shortest exposure to enemy fire.

Lyons readied himself to meet O'Hearn and his men. There was nothing the Konzak could do against the Gun Team until it came closer.

GADGETS AND POL DIDN'T TAKE LONG to figure out they were under fire from two directions. The bullets from down the road snapped angrily over their heads; the mercenaries were shooting high for fear of hitting their own. The hail of lead from the mountain was different. It thudded down around them, hitting the handcuffed prisoners. One was shot in the leg and screamed unendingly.

Politician calmly lined up four smoke grenades for the M-203. He then quickly fired all four, placing them between his position and the troops coming down the mountainside. It placed an effective screen between themselves and the enemy.

Gadgets and Pol moved as the smoke screen was in place, leaving their prisoners behind. It would be only seconds before the enemy made its way through the smoke.

It took O'Hearn and his men several seconds to realize that a lone fighter with blond hair was running toward them.

"Get that son of a bitch!" O'Hearn shouted.

The weapons swung from Gadgets and Pol to bear on Lyons, whose Konzak was well within range. It began its booming oratory in response to the scattered shots from O'Hearn's terrorist-trained mercs.

Two or three bullets embedded themselves in Lyons's flak jacket; several hundred pellets embedded themselves in the enemy. Lyons emptied the clip, yanked it out and rammed home a fresh one. There was a break in the shooting, so he turned and ran for the van. He reached it just as renewed fire broke out from the mountainside.

Politician peeled rubber the instant Lyons had leaped into the back.

"Where are our prisoners?" Lyons demanded.

"We had five," Gadgets told him. "The other side killed most of them accidentally."

"Nice of the Gun Team to clean up for us," Lyons growled. His scowl was ferocious.

Lao said to the chess players, "That break-free was perfectly timed. Had you rehearsed it?"

"No," Pescador replied. "Why would we do that?"

"But you both reacted at precisely the right moment."

"Was there any other logical tactic?" Harju asked.

Lao shook her head.

"You're great people," Pescador said, "but you keep forgetting that we're warriors, too."

"Hah!" Lyons barked.

"We've spent our entire lives studying strategy and tactics," Pescador continued. "Sure, no one gets blasted to bits physically when we do battle—that's the civilized part of chess."

Lyons stared at the young champion for several seconds then laughed. "Okay, warriors. You can be generals anytime you want, but I wouldn't want you as soldiers."

"Why not?"

"You wasted a beat scooping weapons when the retreat was sounded."

Politician took advantage of Lyons's lightened mood to ask, "Where are we headed?"

"The closest military air base, driver. I'm going to arrange our flight to Yugoslavia. The van comes with us. The sooner we get there, the better."

"We'll arrive early."

"Better than arriving dead," Lyons said.

"The flanks are being squeezed, so we're going up the middle," said Pescador. "But I want to know what the hell's happening. Who's after us?"

"Two levels of mercenaries—one level now. But it's anyone's guess who hired them," Lyons said.

Harju and Pescador exchanged glances then shrugged.

"We leave the battlefield for Yugoslavia, until we figure out who we're fighting," Lyons told them.

"You think we'll be safer there?" Harju queried incredulously.

"Can you be less safe than this?" Lyons countered. "On the flight we'll have time to get prepared for battle. Yugoslavia is one place I don't want to be without weapons."

10

The uniform of the Yugoslav army officer showed the rank of colonel, but Lyons knew he was dealing with the SDB, the Yugoslav secret police. He was a short man, only five foot nine. His swarthy face looked sad; the soft brown eyes looked positively doleful. Even his pencil mustache seemed to droop with the sadness of his message.

"I am sorry, Mr. Lyons, but our measurements tell us that your van is riddled with secret compartments, and so we must impound it for the length of your stay here. Rather than tear it apart to see what may be hidden in it, we prefer simply to hold on to it and return it when you leave. A more civilized solution, do you not think?"

"I'm sorry, Colonel, but I didn't get your name."

Lyons knew he was dealing with an experienced professional. The clipped English told of an Oxford education. The authority told of a man versed in the use of power.

"Obilich. Colonel Xerxes Obilich, at your service."

"Your men will find weapons in the van's secret compartments," Lyons said.

"They will be there safely when you leave the country, but why are you telling me this? I made a point of not asking. You are with the American chess players, and we wish to avoid an incident."

Lyons delivered one of his frosty smiles. "Two of the United States's contingent have already been killed. There have been two attempts to kill the other two. That's why we arrived so early.''

"You wished to escape the American terrorists?''

Lyons didn't bother arguing terminology. "Something like that. The bastards might follow us.''

Obilich flashed his white teeth. "Please, sir, do not be offensive. Do you think we take lightly our obligations to protect our guests?''

"No offense intended. I'm doing my job.''

"You must do it unarmed. We found extremely advanced bulletproof . . . uh, underwear, for lack of a better word, in your baggage. You must be content with being a human shield. However, I shall assign men to watch your party at all times. How many need watching?''

"Two players, one coach.''

"Then there are three on the chess team and three guards in your party. Is that correct?''

Lyons nodded. He hoped Pol knew enough chess to pass himself off as a coach. As such, Lyons knew, he would enjoy far more freedom than would a mere bodyguard.

"Very well. Let us leave it like that. Please do not forget that we will be keeping both a protective and restrictive eye on your party.''

Obilich rose, offering his hand. Lyons accepted the handshake then went to round up the rest of the group. He felt incomplete without his weapons: that didn't matter. Keeping the two American players safe while helping the two Russians escape: that mattered.

The six of them were driven in an army transport to the Hotel Excelsior, a modern luxury hotel. They were given two suites of rooms. The smaller suite had a common sitting room and a bedroom each for Lao and Harju. The larger one simply had larger rooms. Lyons arranged to bunk with Pescador, leaving Pol to share a room with Gadgets.

In case the rooms were bugged, they confined their conversation to trivialities. Lyons set the tone by pumping Pescador about generalship on the chessboard. But the weaponless situation called for a conference; so as soon as they were unpacked, they left their rooms and went downstairs.

In the lobby two young men and a young lady, all wearing uniform, came through the door, breathing hard from a quick run, and approached Ironman.

"Mr. Lyons, I am Vanessa. I speak English good. Colonel Obilich sent me. We are to keep an eye on you and see that no harm comes to you during your stay. Colonel says either we follow you around like faithful dogs or we join your party as guides. The choice, it is up to you."

Noticing Lyons flush with anger, Pol stepped forward. "That was considerate of the colonel," he said. "We were about to explore the old city. Won't you join us?"

The nine of them left the hotel and strolled through the old sea gate into the best preserved walled city in the world. Inside, there was no vehicular traffic; the roads between the three-story buildings were too narrow for traffic, but fine for pedestrians. Pol and Lyons took the lead. Lao strolled alongside one of the Yugoslav males, signalling that Harju should do the same. Pescador walked with Vanessa, a paratrooper and antiterror specialist. He didn't mind at all.

"No traffic. This would be a great place for our morning runs," Pescador commented to Harju. Both chess players ran at least three miles daily to keep in shape. Able Team usually ran with them, both to protect them and as part of their own daily fitness routine.

On that first visit to the old city, Lao managed to stop and look around often enough for Lyons and Pol to establish a lead and talk without being overheard and without appearing as though they were trying to do just that. They stayed close enough to the group to cause the guards no alarm.

"How bad is it?" Pol asked.

"The van's impounded until we leave. The extra guards are supposed to replace our weapons. This Obilich is smart and well educated—a diplomat. Wants things to go smoothly. I'd rather cross a roomful of raving maniacs."

"Good, huh?"

"Believe it."

They walked in silence for a while, Politician giving Ironman time to think things through.

"We'll have to play it his way," Lyons decided. "When we hear from the two Russian defectors, we'll make plans. By the way, you're now the chess coach and second; Gadgets, Ti, and I are bodyguards. You'll have to see what the security is around the van. We may have to crack it loose."

They continued in silence while Politician thought over the situation.

"I got an idea. I'll pretend to suffer from periodic fits of deafness. Start shouting at me like I can't hear so good. Then put in a request for me to get stuff from the van. Under supervision, of course."

"You thinking of that hearing aid we use as a listening device? That should get you to the van."

Pol nodded. "And maybe I can sneak out the communicators as well. How about that? I might just turn out to be the best chess coach you ever saw."

"That shouldn't be hard. I've only seen one. Quinn was rotten, but he didn't deserve to die that way. Neither did Kerr."

"It's not your fault, Carl."

"Maybe, but it was my responsibility."

During the walk and the stops at cafés and shops, they managed to change walking partners in a way that seemed spontaneous and allowed Lyons to disseminate his information and solidify the planning.

Once they were back at the hotel, there was no difficulty arranging for Pol to be escorted to the van. The soldiers with him were intrigued with the secret cache of electronics materials. They examined the hearing aid and three communicators Pol took from a hidden compartment. The four objects were forwarded to Obilich before being approved.

For Able Team, the chess players and their Yugoslav guards, the next day began with an early morning run through the nearly deserted streets of the walled city, where they discovered at least one exception to the "no vehicle" rule.

Just after dawn on that spring day, garbage trucks rumbled and clanked through the narrow streets. Only on the Placa, the main street, could two trucks squeeze past each other. In the narrow alleys the trucks filled the roads completely. The occasional pedestrian was forced to step into a doorway to let a truck pass. The garbage vehicles could not negotiate corners without slow, painstaking maneuvers.

They had experienced no trouble importing the computer, which had been listed as a training device and looked like a common portable computer. Lao had rebuilt it from the ground up, but that didn't show on the outside. Over breakfast she announced that her chess program was ready to play Pescador.

Once they had arrived in Yugoslavia, Harju and Pescador underwent a noticeable change in personality: they ate, slept and breathed chess. They were warriors about to enter the arena, and they shut other concerns out of their minds.

For the first games, Politician, wearing a hearing aid, claimed the second's spot immediately behind Pescador.

It was a difficult game. By the endgame, the only advantage the computer had was a slightly better pawn structure. It capitalized on the small advantage, slowly building it into a better king position and more advanced pawns. When the advantage extended to the superiority of one pawn, Pescador resigned.

"Congratulations!" he told Lao. "I really didn't think you could do it."

She accepted his hand and grinned at him. "There's more to it than that."

Politician interrupted. "Normally, the position would have been adjourned after the fortieth move. Let's go to my room and analyze from that point."

Pescador looked puzzled but got up to follow.

"This I've got to see," Harju exclaimed as she followed Pescador.

As Pol set up the board, he said, "As your coach and second, I'm the only one legally allowed to help you analyze your adjourned games. Let's see what I can do for you here."

He played out the next two moves of the game. "Up to this point you were doing all right, but here you should have moved your king toward center."

Pescador gave a snort of laughter. "And abandon my pawn?"

"You play the computer's side. Anne, you help him. He'll need it."

The two champions conferred and moved, certain of a quick win. When Pol had his king among their pawns, they were looking for any win. Finally they agreed they couldn't find a draw.

"How—" Pescador began.

Pol put his finger to his lips.

" . . . about a coffee?" Pescador finished.

The three found the rest of Able Team in the sitting room and the three guides in the lobby. The idea of coffee evolved into a decision to have lunch. Picking a restaurant some distance from the hotel was their best guarantee against an electronic bug in their borscht.

DYNAMITE OFFER

4 EXPLOSIVE NOVELS PLUS A QUARTZ WATCH FREE

delivered right to your home with no obligation to buy — ever

TAKE 'EM FREE

4 action-packed novels and a digital quartz watch

With an offer like this, how can you lose?

Return the attached card, and we'll send you 4 adventure novels just like the one you're reading plus a digital quartz calendar watch—ABSOLUTELY FREE.

If you like them, we'll send you 6 books every other month to preview. Always before they're available in stores. Always for less than the retail price. Always with the right to cancel and owe nothing.

NON-STOP HIGH-VOLTAGE ACTION

As a Gold Eagle subscriber, you'll get the fast-paced, hard-hitting action you crave. Razor-edge stories stripped to their lean muscular essentials. Written in a no-holds-barred style that keeps you riveted from cover to cover.

In addition you'll receive...

- our free newsletter AUTOMAG with every shipment

- special books to preview free and buy at a deep discount

RUSH YOUR ORDER TO US TODAY

Don't let this bargain get away. Send for your 4 free books and wristwatch now. They're yours to keep even if you never buy another Gold Eagle book.

Digital quartz watch keeps you right on time

Unbeatable! That's the word for this tough water-resistant timepiece. Easy-to-read LCD display beams exact time, date and running seconds with flawless quartz precision. Full one-year warranty (excluding battery).

FREE BOOKS & WATCH

YEAH, send my 4 **free** Gold Eagle novels plus my **free** watch. Then send me 6 brand-new Gold Eagle novels (2 **Mack Bolans** and one each of **Phoenix Force, Able Team, Track** and **SOBs**) every second month as they come off the presses. Bill me at the low price of $2.25 each (for a total of $13.50 per shipment—a saving of $1.50 off the retail price). There are no shipping, handling or other hidden charges. I can always return a shipment and cancel at any time. Even if I never buy a book from Gold Eagle, the 4 free books and the watch (a $29.95 value) are mine to keep.

166 CIM PAHU

Name _____ (PLEASE PRINT)

Address _____ Apt. No.

City _____ State/Prov. _____ Zip/Postal Code

Offer limited to one per household and not valid for present subscribers. Prices subject to change.

JOIN FORCES WITH GOLD EAGLE'S HEROES

- Mack Bolan...lone crusader against the Mafia and KGB
- Able Team...3-man combat squad blitzes global terrorism
- Phoenix Force...5 mercenaries battle international crime
- Track...weapons genius stalks madman around the world
- SOBs...avengers of justice from Vietnam to Iran

For free offer, detach and mail

Pescador and Harju isolated Politician from the guides, and Pescador asked, "Okay, give. How did you prepare such an elaborate analysis in no time flat?"

"I'm kind of hard of hearing, but I can still hear Ti's computer."

"If that thing you're wearing is really a radio, how come the police let you keep it?"

"It's really a sensitive hearing aid, no built-in radio. I can't help if if the communicator in my inside jacket pocket is right next to the hearing aid amplifier clipped onto my shirt pocket, causing it to pick up signals by induction."

They laughed and settled down to the serious business of eating the steaming bowls of soup that the waiter had set before them. As they were returning to the hotel, Lyons challenged Pescador, "You call me a warrior because I carry a gun. You call yourself a warrior because you use martial planning when you play games. What's a warrior?"

The American champion mulled over the question before responding, "Yes, I call us both warriors, but not for the reasons you give. To me, a warrior is someone who tries to adapt himself to reality. He dedicates his life to freeing himself from the limitations of his own thought patterns."

"I don't adapt to reality. If I don't like it, I change it," Lyons responded.

"In life, as in chess, we cannot move the opposing pieces. We can only adjust ourselves, our own pieces."

Lyons let out a short bark of a laugh. "Next, you'll be telling me terrorists place themselves in front of my bullets."

Pescador shrugged. "That's exactly what they do. Think about it."

Lao butted into the conversation. "He's too Oriental for me, but he's right."

Lyons brooded for a while.

"Explain," he demanded a minute later.

"You've already figured it out. You have set your own course. It is your decision to fight terrorism. A person who undertakes terrorist activities makes his own decision, arranges the pieces of his life to suit himself. When he or she is lined up in your sights and you pull the trigger, that death is by mutual agreement. So, I say yes, the terrorist places himself in line with your bullets."

"But he doesn't want to die," Lyons said.

"If he's human, he's already dead."

Lyons laughed. "No argument from me."

"I'm not sure I understand it," Politician said.

Pescador explained, "A person who kills others is either an animal who puts no value on human life, or a warrior. Shooting a rabid dog is not a matter of war; it's a matter of mercy. A warrior's already dead; no one kills him. He chose death when he chose the warriors' path."

"What do you mean, 'a warrior's already dead'?" Harju interrupted.

Surprisingly, it was Lyons who answered. "A man who tries to protect his own life isn't effective. The most potent fighters give themselves up as dead then do the most damage they can before they stop moving."

Pescador picked up the explanation. "When you are up against a chess opponent with a better rating, what do you tell yourself?"

Harju hesitated before replying, "That I may get beaten, but my opponent will know she's been in a contest."

"See! You give yourself up for dead."

"I never thought of the enemy creating his own destruction in quite that way, but you're right," Lyons admitted as they walked into the hotel. There was a man at the reception desk, just checking in. Lyons said, "I wonder if he's an animal, a warrior, or both?"

"No man is both," Lao said. "Who is he?"

"Stefan Barazov, Bulgaria's chief export."

"A terrorist?"

"A rabid fox. It's a good thing we're already dead." Lyons's voice had a touch of bitterness, caused by frustration. The assignment was not an easy one.

11

On the first day of the tournament, the Hotel Excelsior looked less like a dignified hostelry than a Roman colosseum on lion-feeding day. The Eastern European press was out in force. There were several journalists from each Western European nation, but only two reporters from all of North America, one from a wire service and one from *Chess Life and Review.*

In the week before the tourney, the weather hadn't been unlike Southern California's in the spring, but on the first day, storm clouds gathered and rain periodically drenched the city.

For the first time since coming to Dubrovnik, Able Team and its charges didn't enjoy their early morning fitness run through the walled city.

Pol introduced himself to the tournament director as the coach and second to both U.S. players. The director, a Norwegian with a good command of English and half a dozen other languages, treated him with cold formality.

Blancanales quickly found that the world of championship chess was much like a small village. The people might not like one another, but they knew all about one another. A stranger was an impostor until proven otherwise. Surprisingly, the least hostility came from the Russians, who seemed more curious than the others.

Pol caught his first glimpse of Kubasov and Tsigal, the two Russians who planned to defect to the United States.

They were milling with the other Communist bloc players, not hanging back and not paying undue attention to Americans.

Igor Kubasov looked like a college professor. Tall, thin, with an unruly mass of gray hair, he wore a sport jacket, knit vest, white shirt and tie.

Manolis Tsigal was still in his midtwenties. As thin but not as tall as Kubasov, he was the type of person most people would describe as intense. His head was a mass of short black curly hair; his mustache was both black and bushy. He wore jeans, an open-necked shirt and a light knit sweater.

To Politician's surprise, Nicholai Zhdanov, the retired world champion, was also there. Zhdanov, an engineer by trade, had held the world championship, on and off, for longer than anyone. He had retired, both from chess and from his job, over ten years ago.

He had become interested in computer development, especially computers that could simulate human thought or play chess. He'd gone back to work on his pet project. Now he had come to play America's newest chess-playing computer. He wouldn't be out of shape: he'd been coaching other world champions since his retirement.

Pol turned as Pescador approached.

"Did you see who I drew for the first round?" the U.S. champion demanded, scowling.

Pol shook his head.

"Tsigal, damn it!"

"So?"

"So he clobbered me the last two times we played. It's a hell of a way to begin a tournament."

"That was five years ago. You'd just made your International Master points."

"How did you know that?"

"I've been doing my homework. If I'm going to act as your second, I'm going to do a job of it."

Pescador gave him a sad smile and shook his head. "Can't be done. They've seen through you already."

"What do you mean?"

"Chess is a closed shop. All the players know all the names worth knowing. Blancanales just isn't one of those names."

"Then you and Harju are going to have to educate them."

They walked over to where Harju was talking to a woman from the Communist bloc. When they were able to talk without being overheard, Pol moved straight to the point.

"I need both of you to help establish my chess reputation as quickly as possible. That means you're going to have to lend me your glory."

"It won't work," Harju interrupted.

"Is that how long it takes you to decide the value of a gambit?" Pol snapped back.

She hadn't heard the only diplomatic member of Able Team speak with anger before. It brought her up short. There was a moment's hesitation then Harju smiled.

"Sorry. What did you have in mind?"

"Thanks to Lao's computer, you're both better prepared than before. You've both improved on your own. I want you to give me the credit, by refusing to discuss me at all."

There was a pause.

"I'm not sure I understand," Harju said.

"No one's ever heard of me. We have to make them all believe that's the way we want it. Refuse to answer questions. If someone says I'm merely a security guard, agree. Confide only to close friends that I really am a coach but refuse to elaborate."

The two looked blank.

Then Harju grinned. "By making it look like we don't want anyone to take you seriously, we raise questions," she said.

"You're getting it. One more thing. It's not completely fair of me to ask, but it's necessary for my cover. When you win, run to me. I'm the first person whose approval you want. Got that?"

"It just might work. Why are we going to all this trouble?" Pescador asked.

Harju answered for Pol. "It's a gambit, idiot. If we can convince people that we're improving because of our secret coach, the killers are more apt to go after him than us."

"I'm not sure it'll work, but it's worth a try," Pol added.

Determined to surround Pol with an aura of mysterious knowledge, the two wandered away to greet more fellow chess players.

A Hungarian master by the name of Gruda was the first to approach Pol directly. The chess player was elderly and had an excellent command of English.

"I don't believe we've met," Gruda said, offering his hand.

Pol shook his hand, studying the man's face. "But your fame precedes you, Mr. Gruda. I'm Rosario Blancanales."

Gruda got straight to the point. "I thought young Mr. Quinn was coaching the Americans."

Pol decided to use bluntness as a weapon. "He was killed in an attempt to stop my protégés from coming here. So, of course, I was forced to take his place."

"Forced?"

"No one else knew their training program."

"Then you were an assistant to Mr. Quinn?"

"Something like that. Would you like a tip?"

"Help from an American coach would be different. What did you have in mind?"

"If you draw black against Billy, stay away from Philador's defense. I know it's your favorite, but we have an excellent trap prepared."

"Why tell me this?"

"I don't believe good chess is based on surprises. The best chess takes place when the other player knows exactly what you're doing and can't do a thing to stop you."

Gruda laughed. "I see you understand the situation well. Both on and off the board."

He hurried away to talk to the Russians, undoubtedly to report every word of the conversation.

Pescador reappeared at Pol's side. "Did he manage to pump you?"

"Certainly did. I told him you had a trap prepared for him, if he played his favorite Philador's against you."

Pescador's face fell for a moment then he laughed. "Beautiful. The old codger won't be able to resist, now. You should have been a chess player."

"I am. Now."

The pair of them looked so confident as they laughed that many eyes in the room darted toward them.

Meanwhile, Harju was approached by an old friend, the coach and second for the Russian women's team; she wouldn't dare be seen talking to Harju unless the KGB had told her to. Several KGB operatives always traveled with the chess players.

"Anne, how is life in America?" she asked in Russian.

"Not as orderly as in Russia."

"You're not happy, then?"

"Lonely, but I savor the freedom."

Nadezhda decided it would be safer to change the subject. "You have a new coach, I see."

"Sort of."

"What do you mean 'sort of'?"

"Nothing. Nothing. I've known Rosario ever since I escaped. That's all."

The Russian coach changed the subject again, but Harju was sure the idea of a secret coach would soon be firmly planted in Russian minds.

The first games went well. A Russian was paired against the Little General and lost. Anne had an easy first round in the women's section. But the game between Tsigal and Pescador was the most interesting of the afternoon.

The moves were made quickly. At the twentieth move Pescador varied his response with a highly speculative move. When the dust finally settled, Pescador had a bishop for a pawn. Tsigal resigned. Pescador's fighting style was the talk of the tournament.

Gadgets and Ironman roamed the area, but Russian security seemed to be less than expected. The unpleasant jolt for the day came when Lyons spotted a male journalist who sported long blond hair.

"We need weapons," Lyons told Gadgets.

"Sure."

"Cannibal's over there in the press corps, wearing a yellow rug. Want to bet the rest of his animals aren't close by?"

"No bet. Hope he had as much trouble with his weapons as we had with ours."

"Want to quote odds?"

Gadgets shook his head.

The next day Pescador found himself in a rough game. It was adjourned after the fortieth move, but Pescador had no edge. Harju was in even more difficulties in her adjourned game. The attention of all the players and seconds was riveted on Politician. The adjournment analyses were expected to reveal him for a fake and to cause the loss of a point for each American.

The two players, Pol, and Lao and her computer held a marathon session. They found a draw for Harju, but Pescador's game seemed to defy analysis.

Finally Lao had an inspiration and fed the preferences of the Russian contingent into the computer. The style program had been meant for the openings, not the endings, but it surprised them. It revealed a pattern in the Russian thinking in queen and pawn endings. By entering only the options that fit the pattern, they discovered several traps for Pescador to set. None of the traps were less than eight moves deep.

Despite the late night, the group was up for its dawn run and an early breakfast before going down to the playing hall. The adjourned games were played in the morning to clear the decks for the next round in the afternoon. Although chess players usually try to sleep or rest if they don't have a game to finish, most of them turned up to watch the two Americans.

Anne played easily to her draw. The Little General finished its second game, winning again.

Pescador didn't have an easy time, but it was exciting. His opponent blundered into the first trap Pescador set. The result was an even game, but the Russian mounted a ferocious and desperate attack.

Pescador defended himself for three grueling hours. When at last he managed to beat back the attack, he found himself with a superior position and converted his potential loss into a brilliant win. When the opponent captured his king, the room broke into applause.

After Pescador won, Gruda congratulated Politician. "Seeing my English is passable, the Russian coaches and seconds have asked me to talk to you. Will you play them a small second's tournament tomorrow? They'd like to get to know you better."

"They'd like to know whether I'm really a chess coach or simply an undercover bodyguard," Pol responded.

"That might be the case. None of us has ever heard of you before. It's nice to know who you're up against."

"I'm simply a bodyguard."

"Then who coaches the Americans to their brilliant finishes for the adjourned games? We know there were only four of you working on it, and we doubt that Oriental woman is the coach."

"I seem to be caught."

"Are you?"

Pol drew a deep breath, studying the Hungarian player. It was time to intensify the bluntness. "I don't have time to spare. I have two people to second. Tell your friends that a tournament is out, but in the interests of friendship, I'll give them a chance to assess my playing strength. Have them appoint three seconds, and I'll play them simultaneously."

"You make a joke, no?"

"No. I mean it."

Gruda left, shaking his head.

Lao's program proved its value again that afternoon. Both Harju and Pescador were well primed on their opponents' playing styles. Both combined the knowledge with their natural abilities and won brilliantly. The entire chess community was crediting the mysterious coach. Whenever the Americans were asked to comment, they simply credited their coach and refused further comment.

When she won another game, Harju put the finishing touch on Politician's build up. After her opponent resigned, she accepted the proffered handshake, reported the result to the scorekeeper then ran full out to the men's tourney room, where Pol happened to be watching Pescador.

She met him with unlimited exuberance and hugged and kissed him. "I did it!" she exclaimed, leaping into the air.

An assistant tournament director immediately shushed her, and she left the room. But she'd established the message more clearly than any words could.

Five minutes later a Russian second told Politician that his challenge had been accepted.

The games, which took place the next morning in a large hospitality room, attracted more insiders than the finishing of the adjourned games. The simultaneous match had been set up with all the attention to detail that had been given to the main tournament. Demonstration boards, to which moves were transferred from the boards on the table so everyone could see, were set up on the walls. Two of the grand masters had agreed to act as tournament directors for Pol's games. For the first time, Pol was fully aware of just how seriously some of the world took chess.

With polite firmness, the players insisted on examining Politician's hearing aid. Pretending mild indignation, he handed it over. They immediately turned it over to Zhdanov, the retired world champion and electronics engineer. He certified it to be an unusual hearing aid, but nevertheless only a hearing aid.

Politician clipped it back on his shirt pocket and Zhdanov resumed his seat in the front row of spectators. With the hearing aid once more under the double-frequency communicator in his jacket pocket, where the two could interact by induction, Lao could again hear what was happening. With a sending unit under her long hair, Harju was standing among the onlookers at the back of the room. It was her job to make sure each opponent's move was relayed to Lao. Pescador was sitting with Lao to help the computer decide Pol's moves.

The games were not without their problems, but the results were exactly what the doctor ordered: two wins and a draw for Pol. Although the seconds weren't the caliber of those participating in the tournament, they were strong players. Pol's reputation as a chess coach of no mean ability seemed to be strongly established.

The last to leave was Zhdanov, who shook Pol's hand and said, "I'll buy you a drink."

Pol was about to politely decline when Zhdanov continued, "We can talk there without being spied upon. You can convince me that the same computer that helped you is not helping the two players you coach."

12

Winston Dangerfield entered his room on the tenth floor of the Hotel Excelsior and then stopped in surprise. A man with long blond hair was sitting in the easy chair, grinning at him.

"Come in, Winston. It really is your room. I simply took the liberty of letting myself in rather than stand waiting around in the hall. How did the Little General do today?"

Dangerfield slammed the door and stepped to the table where he'd set up a small bar to refresh potential buyers of the Little General. He poured himself a Scotch and added some soda from an old-fashioned siphon.

"I'll take a scotch without the splash," Cannibal Jones said. Dangerfield poured the drink and handed the glass to Jones then sat down opposite him.

After a long sip on his own drink, Dangerfield answered the question. "It lost to that English bastard."

"You didn't expect that?"

"Frankly, I didn't. He played them close to his chest and led trumps. We invited him because he's made such a big thing out of playing computers. As soon as he received the invitation, he cabled to make sure we understood that his offer of 10,000 pounds to the first computer to beat him had been withdrawn. It was considered an encouraging sign."

"You were sandbagged."

"That's the bottom line."

"How serious is it?"

"Depends who else beats it. A loss and a couple of draws will still win the tournament. It could conceivably win with two losses and no draws. These grand masters are very close in strength. No one wins with a perfect score."

"But a win by Pescador will put the results in doubt?"

Dangerfield nodded.

"Then he's going to have an accident."

"Won't work. People will immediately know why he had an accident."

"I don't tell you how to build your goddamn computers. Don't tell me how to handle the roadblocks." Jones's voice made Dangerfield shiver.

"I thought you weren't to take any direct part in this. It isn't necessary, and Arma doesn't want this connected with him."

Jones grinned over the top of the glass at the industrialist. "Old Arma still hasn't taught you the rules of the game. You're allowed to use your head. I can take action, if necessary, as long as I'm not caught. I hired other mercs as I was told and unless I can rectify things, I'll be blamed for their stupidity. No one's allowed failure. There aren't any second chances."

"Seems like you got a second chance."

"Took nerve for you to say that, didn't it? You may acquire enough guts to make it yet. So, I'll answer your question. No. We got just one chance as soldiers. Now we got just one chance as the old man's mercenaries. You aren't going to lose that chance for us."

Cannibal Jones slammed his glass down on an end table and stalked out of the room, leaving a white-faced Dangerfield staring after him.

ZHDANOV LED POLITICIAN to a corner of the bar near the television. He ordered drinks and asked the bartender to turn up the volume on the television.

"I think this will have to do as a bug-free environment," the Russian said in his too-precise English. "Now, what do you have to say for yourself?"

The noise forced Politician to turn down the hearing aid, effectively cutting him off from communication with Lao.

"What makes you think there was a computer involved?"

"The noise of the television just forced you to turn down the hearing aid. Yet you hear me?"

Politician nodded.

"But I wasn't wrong about that hearing aid. It's not a receiver."

"Only by induction." Politician produced the communicator from his belt and put it to his lips.

"Say something to Nicholai Zhdanov," he said into the communicator then handed it to the engineer and chess master.

Zhdanov listened and handed it back. "Mr. Pescador wished me good health. A clever trick, but you have made no answer to my question."

Politician sipped his beer. He was in a delicate spot. Zhdanov seemed genuinely curious and concerned only that the tournament was not rigged. Pol would have liked to consult the rest of the team but sensed that frank dealing and no small measure of trust was the only way around the dilemma.

"What makes you believe a computer's involved?" Pol repeated.

Zhdanov sipped his mineral water while he considered the question. Two men whom Pol recognized as KGB types came into the bar and tried to join them. The chess master waved them away. They took a table where they could watch without overhearing anything.

"They seem to trust you," Pol commented.

Zhdanov seemed happy to change the topic of conversation. "They have no reason not to. I understand the restrictiveness of our system. I am a peasant at heart. I would never be happy away from the motherland. The system is not just. No system is. But it has been kind to me. I have a wife. Married forty years. Nothing could induce me to leave her and our home. No, unlike some of our group, I am safe."

The talking seemed to bring him to a decision. He took another sip of his water then said, "You have answered my major concern most well. If Pescador and Harju do not wear hearing aids, they are not being coached at the table. Away from the table, there are still no rules against computer assistance. It has never mattered before. I will tell you what I have surmised and see what you do with it."

"You don't play chess by any chance? I see you'd be good at it," Pol quipped.

The ex-world champion chuckled heartily. "Let's see how well you handle the next move.

"Computers do not think like people. They lack intuition and a sense of beauty. Intuition and a sense of beauty are most important to the making of a great chess player. He must feel the position in his soul.

"Computers have almost no positional sense. They follow a few general rules, but make up for it by mechanically sorting through more possibilities than the human mind can handle. Your play today was mechanical. Occasionally Billy Pescador saved your position, but on the whole you relied on brute computing power to win those games. They were not beautiful. I didn't know how you did it, but I was as certain you used a computer as if you tried to pass typewriting off as handwriting. Do I make myself clear?"

"Extremely."

Zhdanov paused to consider the rest of his speech then continued. "I have surmised a great deal more than this. I will tell you the rest of it.

"Why, I ask myself, should such professional people bother to fake an ability at chess? You are not one of those people who need to fake greatness because you have none of your own. I have heard the talk. I know that people have been trying to kill the American chess players. But the bodyguards are more than bodyguards, and the chess coach may not be a chess coach, but he is a distinguished warrior. I think he is part of the team of warriors who pretend to be bodyguards."

Politician had no answer to Zhdanov's speculations. So he said nothing.

"I know why you're really here," the Russian said.

ESENIN DIDN'T RISK meeting Barazov in a public bar. Instead, taking due precautions not to be seen, he went to Barazov's room.

"I've been expecting you ever since I checked in," Barazov said in English. The Bulgarian terrorist's Russian was passable, but he preferred not to give the KGB agent the advantage of working in his own language.

Esenin's grin was about as reassuring as the beckoning hand of Death.

"You're not my only worry, Stefan. I'm concerned how well our American capitalist is bearing up. As you are undoubtedly aware, that American chess player and the damn defector survived both an attempt to kidnap them and two attempts to eliminate them entirely. They're posing a problem."

"And what do you want me to do about it?"

Esenin sighed. "Are you all set for the final day?"

"Of course. I'm simply staying here to monitor the situation, to make sure it doesn't change. In two days, loyal freedom fighters in American-made fatigues, using cheap American-made weapons, will steal the computer and kidnap two hostages—Kubasov and Harju. Kubasov will be found dead, Harju will never be seen again, and some computer wreckage will be found."

Esenin paused, reluctant to introduce the next topic of conversation. "How difficult would it be to arrange an accident before then?"

Barazov laughed. He had a flashing handsomeness when he laughed, but no warmth.

"You're not going to import some American gangsters for another try at Pescador?"

Esenin ignored the dig. "It must be an accident, beyond all doubt. How much?"

"I thought you KGB types were the experts: gases that simulate heart attacks, drugs that cause strokes."

"Never mind the sarcasm. The Americans may be on to those tricks, but soon we have some new ones. In the meantime, how much?"

"In dollars or rubles?"

"Rubles."

"It's always more costly in rubles."

"Never mind the buildup. Can you do it? How much?"

"Of course I can do it. Cost you twelve hundred rubles anywhere else. Double that because we're in a Warsaw Pact country."

"Only three thousand in American dollars? Why so cheap?"

"I would have charged you only two thousand, if you paid in American dollars. It is a simple job. Why should I charge more?"

"You are intent on ruining my reputation with my superior, trying to make it seem that I have paid too much for services not delivered."

"Anything you paid was too much. The American gangsters failed to deliver."

Esenin answered with his cold grin. "You have the job. Make sure Pescador is not around to beat that computer. Make sure no one ever suspects that is the reason he's not around."

"It will be a strike against American imperialists in general, but I am curious. What do you care about the American computer? The Soviet copy will never be associated with it."

"If we bring this off for the company, we own them. Surely that is clear. They will have to keep us up to date from here on."

Barazov nodded. "You always think deeply, Esenin. Perhaps you could beat the computer."

"At chess? No. But at strategic planning, I'm doing just that. Do you think that American is not using his computer to try to outmaneuver me? I shall beat both him and his machine."

Barazov grinned. "Just because we're paranoid doesn't mean the computer isn't out to get us."

A TALL BLOND MAN with cold eyes entered the bar and sat close to the two KGB agents who were watching Zhdanov talking to Politician at the bar.

As the two KGB men stood up to move over to the bar, the blond man reached over and yanked them back into their chairs.

"I insist on buying you a drink," Lyons told them loudly, his voice carrying to Politician and Zhdanov.

Zhdanov glanced over at the KGB agents then back to Politician and picked up the conversation.

"It stands to reason. The party regulars have been stung by the defections of top players, first Korchnoi, now Spassky plays for France. There are two of our number who stand to lose most of their freedom, because their ties to the motherland have weakened. It seems logical a team of your caliber would be sent to help them do just that."

"And how would you feel about it?"

The ex-champion shrugged. "I cannot understand. I could never desert my country. I could never be driven out by overzealous party hacks. But if that is the foolishness they choose, I believe they should be free to choose it. I'd neither help nor interfere."

Politician felt no release of tension. Could he trust the crafty old Russian? Pol reflected wryly that he had little choice.

Zhdanov finished his mineral water, wished Pol good luck, collected the two furious KGB operatives and left. Pol and Ironman headed back to their suite.

THE DAY DAWNED, CLEAN AND CRISP. The sun was not yet over the mountains, but the sky had already lightened to a pale blue. All six were happy to run again through the walled city, whose cobbled streets were broken only by the occasional flight of stairs.

Ahead of Gadgets, Lao, Harju and Pescador, Politician carried his walking stick in his left hand; Lyons carried fifty pounds of sand in a backpack, "just to make the run interesting." Vanessa and the two other Yugoslav guards followed. They were specially trained for stamina and endurance but had to push to keep up.

A large rattling garbage truck suddenly appeared behind the group. Two men in coveralls rode the runningboards on each side of the cab; four more clung to posts in the rear. The truck didn't stop at the first pile of garbage. Instead the driver stomped on the accelerator, and the truck picked up speed.

Lyons's ears were the first to pick up the wrong note of the whining engine.

"Around the corner. Fast!" Lyons bellowed as he unslung his backpack and stepped into a doorway, followed by the others.

The three Yugoslav soldiers needed no second warning. Putting on short bursts of speed, the two males managed to stumble into doorways. Vanessa, the female paratrooper, demonstrated astonishing agility. The truck bumper just grazed her backside as she powered around the corner of a building.

In the narrow streets the truck had to slow drastically to make the turn. In trying to rush it, the driver scraped fenders on two walls. The difficulty with the tight turns gave the runners their best advantage.

The two terrorists riding the runningboards didn't dare try jumping clear of the truck. They would have simply bounced off a wall and landed under the wheels. But the four riding the back of the truck all leaped clear to take care of those who had escaped by stepping into doorways.

The Yugoslav soldiers drew their Zastava Model 70s. They had wisely reworked the Soviet Tokarev to take 9 mm parabellums instead of the Soviet standard 7.62 cartridge. Exactly 200 mm long, the small automatics weighed a full kilogram. The box magazine held nine rounds.

The soldiers were well trained and had no lack of courage, but they had a fatal lack of experience. One barked something in his own language, probably a demand that their attackers drop their Kalashnikovs.

Two of the men in coveralls replied instantly with sustained bursts of fire that turned the young soldier into a mass of bloody meat.

The other male soldier didn't waste time: he took a firing-range stance and pumped bullets into one terrorist. The latter died, but not before his AK ripped the brave inexperienced Yugoslav from crotch to neck.

The fourth attacker turned toward Lyons, who was rushing him with the sack of sand held in front of him. The first shots went wide; the next few dug into sand. Then Lyons's sandbag hit the terrorist's gunhand, forcing the weapon to one side. One hundred ninety pounds of ferocious warrior plus fifty pounds of sand slammed the killer across the narrow street to crash against the stone wall of a house.

The two remaining terrorists whirled toward Lyons, their fingers still on the triggers of the AKs. But they had already spent their magazines on the dead soldiers. The first omen of their impending deaths was when they squeezed the triggers of their AKs and nothing happened.

Then Ironman was there, fulfilling prophecy. He went right through the two. A fist like a battering ram smashed chest bone, sending splinters into one terrorist's lungs. A sweeping roundhouse kick caught the other terrorist in the solar plexus, temporarily paralyzing both the respiration and blood circulation.

That terrorist was just pulling himself erect off the wall of the house when Lyons delivered a quick series of kicks and punches. The man collapsed with a dislocated knee, two broken ribs and a broken neck. He was now nothing more than the garbage he had been pretending to collect.

Lyons spun around to greet the last two terrorists, who had finally jumped from the side of the garbage truck. He kicked one in the solar plexus, disabling him. Lyons's combat boot snapped the thug's neck. The last man tried to draw a knife. A kick to the crotch lifted him off his feet and left him in the narrow street for the police to pick up when they removed the human rubbish.

Lyons picked up two of the AKs. Each had a smooth grip in front without a dropped handle. The metal plate over the bolt was grooved. Lyons recognized the Bulgarian manufacture of the weapons.

He did a lightning search for clips and gathered up the dead soldier's unfired Zastava and six full magazines for the AKs. He slammed home fresh magazines in both the AKs, tucked the extra clips into his belt then took off after the garbage truck. Lyons ran full out, his feet barely touching the pavement; his body seemed to float as if rocket propelled.

When the attack had begun, Gadgets led Politician, Lao, Harju and Pescador and the female paratrooper into the next cross street, where they found shelter and prepared for battle.

Pol was pressed against a wall four feet from the corner. As the garbage truck inched around the corner, he jumped outward and thrust twice with the *jo*. Each hard thrust went through the grill and penetrated the rad core. He zigzagged away to make it difficult for the two on the runningboards to aim with their Kalashnikovs.

The truck lumbered on, but in the winding streets it lacked the maneuvering ability of the joggers. The runners reached the next corner ahead of the garbage truck, and rounded it to what they thought was safety.

That was when another garbage truck turned into the street from the far end.

13

As the truck put on a burst of speed, Gadgets barked orders to the runners who fell into single file. Spaced about six feet apart, they jogged slowly to meet the onrushing vehicle. Behind them the other truck had rounded the corner and was accelerating toward them.

Leading the file of joggers, Gadgets kept his eye on the truck ahead. He could make out the two faces in the cab. The Gun Team were on the job once more. Doris Drane, her blond hair barely visible over the top of the steering wheel, drove the truck. Cannibal Jones rode beside her.

When he was less than twenty feet from the front bumper, Gadgets dived to the cobblestones, lying parallel to the houses and in the exact center of the street. Behind him the rest of the group imitated his move. The timing was so close that the truck coming from the rear passed over Politician just as the onrushing truck went over Gadgets.

The high old trucks cleared the line of bodies with inches to spare. The drivers tried to swerve the vehicles to crush their targets beneath the wheels, but the street was too narrow, and the attempt had made Doris Drane scrape the left side of her truck. The other driver was more cautious, remembering the riders on the runningboards.

Each driver assumed the other would be the first to put on the brakes. Their trucks met with a resounding crash. The Bulgarian terrorists who had been riding the running-boards and manipulating their subguns with their free hands were pitched off their perches. Three members of the Gun Team, riding the back of the truck they had stolen, momentarily lost their balance.

Gadgets rose as soon as the Gun Team truck passed over him. He yanked Slaughter Smith's Beretta M92-SB from him in the confusion and covered all three of them with it.

O. D. Yus and Fatheringham had both been riding with their automatics in their hands. No one was particularly anxious to start the shooting. They remained frozen in a two-to-one, Mexican standoff.

After the trucks collided, Politician leaped to his feet, prepared to do battle. So was one of the runningboard riders who had rolled into a doorway without losing his weapon. Crouching, he worked the bolt and brought up the assault rifle, searching for a target just as Politician presented himself.

Pol threw himself at the wall, out of the direct line of fire. Even as he launched himself, he heard a short burst of autofire.

Meanwhile, Harju and Pescador turned to the side of the trucks closest to the wall. The terrorist who had been riding the runningboard on that side had spun off and become wedged between a wall and the front fender of the Gun Team truck. Both chess players moved toward him.

Managing to extricate himself, the terrorist started to turn, only to feel hands grab his boots. He lost his balance and fell back between the truck and the building. Before he could move, the two young people were on him. He bucked and heaved, but there was no room to maneuver.

Pescador grabbed the Kalashnikov, taking it out of play. He put as much of his weight as he could manage on the terrorist's chest, keeping the man pinned.

This left Harju with the perplexing job of subduing the terrorist's thrashing legs. She dug her fingers into calf muscle, but he began to kick with his other leg. Slowly, ignoring the short kicks from the free leg, she sank her teeth into his muscular thigh.

The terrorist yelled. Pescador took advantage of the distraction to shove the assult rifle across the upper chest of the terrorist's body as both men struggled for possession.

Straining, the terrorist gained the most leverage on the weapon and was using it to slowly pry Pescador off his chest. The Bulgarian had fifty more pounds of muscle than the chess player and used it to advantage. He released the rifle with one hand and drove his fist into the chess player's ribs.

Seeing that the big man's blows were telling on Pescador, Harju was about to throw herself farther up the terrorist's body, when she found her shoulders squeezed between his two powerful legs. She had no choice but to bite through the fabric of the twill pants. Her teeth clamped down on his crotch.

The terrorist screamed, releasing his grip on the AK for just long enough for Pescador to slide it up another four inches and start to bear down on it as it lay across the Bulgarian's windpipe.

While Harju and Pescador struggled, the Yugoslav paratrooper named Vanessa drew her Zastava and turned to crawl from under the Bulgarian-driven vehicle. She saw a boot descend from the truck and fired at the ankle, but her shot was off and simply nicked the heel. There was a bellow of pain and the boot was withdrawn into the cab.

Still beneath the truck, she swung the automatic at a terrorist who was propped in a doorway. The Bulgarian killer was bringing his AK to bear on someone she couldn't see. She steadied the Model 70 and squeezed the trigger. A two-round burst ruined the terrorist's aim by boring into his right eye. The second shot saved the undertaker the task of parting the hair.

The two Bulgarians in the cab of the truck jumped out and immediately rolled under the truck, out of the lines of fire. The blond paratrooper took her eye from the sights and found herself staring at two Tokarevs.

AFTER ANNIHILATING THE TERRORISTS, Lyons followed the Bulgarian-driven garbage truck, pushing his long legs for every ounce of thrust they could give as he watched the explosive action unfold before him.

He saw Politician's attempt at an end run come up short, saw Harju and Pescador manhandle the terrorist, recognized Cannibal Jones as he put a leg down and practically lost his foot, saw the would-be assassin crumple from bullets fired from under the truck. Then he saw the two terrorists jump from the cab and roll under the truck at about the same place from where the friendly fire had originated.

As he ran, he raised the AK and fired a short burst at the windshield of the far truck. The burst was a few inches high and took out the top three inches of the windshield. A second later the truck started to back away. Soon it was backing up as fast as the narrow street would permit.

From several directions came the undulating wails of police sirens.

Ironman needed to be at ground level fast. He took a two-handed grip on the AK, then without breaking stride, dived headfirst at the side of the truck. At the last moment he pivoted so that the back of his right shoulder was the first point to touch the ground. It scraped the pavement, shredding cloth and skin, causing a moderate abrasion that he ignored. His forward dive turned into a sideways roll, and he was under the garbage truck, lying across the legs of two startled terrorists.

Both gunmen twisted in fright, swinging their weapons around.

The barrel of Lyons's AK touched the ear of one terrorist. Ironman pulled the trigger. Quarters were too camped to draw a bead on the second killer. Lyons simply swung the gun barrel, grinding the huge front sight in an eye socket. The Bulgarian's high scream was cut short by a 9 mm squelch control from Vanessa's Model 70.

Lyons spared one glance for the struggle between the chess players and the terrorist. There was no room to maneuver on that side of the truck, so he rolled out the same side as he'd rolled under. He was on his feet in a moment. That was when he saw Gadgets lying in the middle of the road.

Gadgets's Mexican standoff had been interrupted when the garbage truck started to back up. Schwartz threw himself back just as Yus and Fatheringham fired. The bullets snapped over his head.

Before they could again acquire target, the truck was on top of Gadgets, who had lost the M92-SB when he had dived to the ground. Not knowing the nature of the action in front of the truck, the electronics genius stayed motionless until he could spot the automatic. Meanwhile, the truck had rolled away.

Retrieving his gun, Gadgets looked up and saw Lyons towering over him. "If you're through resting, we have a run to finish," Lyons told him.

Gadgets stood up as Lyons began running to the truck. Gadgets scrambled after him. They arrived just in time to see Pescador pressing an AK down on the terrorist's neck while Harju held the choking man's legs. The terrorist gave a last spastic kick and went limp. Pescador didn't stand up until he was certain the man was unconscious and not faking. He turned and saw Lyons do something he seldom did.

Lyons threw Pescador and Harju a friendly salute.

Small Fiat-built police cars swarmed over the area, followed by two vans containing special police in complete riot gear.

The warriors found themselves covered by enough automatic weapons to hold the Maginot Line. In the interests of international goodwill and personal survival, Able Team decided to drop its weapons.

They were not questioned. No words were spoken, except for a few brief commands to the police from their officers. None of the police impinged on the fire zone to gather the dropped weapons.

Three minutes of tense silence elapsed. Then an unmarked car with a uniformed driver arrived. The other cars were moved to allow the new arrival to drive to the battle area.

Colonel Xerxes Obilich climbed out and quietly surveyed the situation. He wore battle fatigues and sported a Skorpion in a custom-made clip holster.

Obilich beckoned to Vanessa. She walked over to his car and gave him a report. She spoke in a low voice that didn't carry to Able Team. She spoke steadily and unemotionally. Obilich listened with complete concentration.

When Vanessa had finished, Obilich told her in English, in a voice intended to carry to Able Team, "Go and report to the police inspector. He'll need something to put in his report."

Vanessa saluted and walked over to the policeman in command. Obilich beckoned for Lyons to join him. When the Able Team warrior drew close, Obilich eyed the tattered cloth surrounding his bloodied shoulder then looked to Ironman's face.

"It seems as if your trouble followed you from the United States," Obilich began.

Since the police had arrived, Lyons had been preparing for this conversation with Obilich. He decided there was nothing to be gained by being forced to be on the defensive. Harju and Pescador had been too occupied to see who was in the second truck; they'd be in no position to contradict Lyons's story. Obilich had spoken in a natural tone of voice. Lyons knew his partners would pick up enough of the conversation to follow his lead.

"May I pick up the weapon I was holding?" Lyons countered.

"Not to keep."

"Not to keep."

Lyons strode back and stooped for the weapon. He could feel the collective easing of tension when he picked it up by the barrel. He walked back and handed it to Obilich.

"Bulgarian manufacture. Not standard items for the American underworld."

The SDB colonel glanced at the weapon and nodded. Lyons noted a tightening of his jaw muscles.

The silence stretched taut before Obilich asked, "What about the men in the second truck?"

"You mean you haven't apprehended them?"

"Mr. Lyons, please allow me to ask the questions."

"For now. What about the men in the other truck?"

"Were they Bulgarians also?"

"It seems a natural assumption. I didn't get a chance to ask them."

"I get the feeling you're not cooperating. What are you holding back?"

"Anger."

"Directed at me?"

"Directed at you."

"For not allowing you your weapons. You have not lost any of your party. I've lost two good soldiers. I understand I should have lost three if it weren't for you. For that I thank you."

Another siren drew closer.

"It works out. She may have saved one of ours. She's a good warrior. The anger is because we were the ones attacked, yet we're being held at gunpoint, like criminals. We didn't bring this trouble with us; it's been manufactured locally."

Obilich turned as another unmarked car pulled up, its siren wailing. "That will be the doctor for your shoulder. I presumed you wouldn't allow us to take you to the hospital. I promise to listen further to your complaints when he's through."

Lyons shook his head. "We can talk while he works. Time matters. Can the rest of the group get back to the hotel for a shower and breakfast? And what are you doing about their security, now?"

"You *are* a problem, Mr. Lyons. I suppose you have some firm ideas regarding what you'll accept?"

"It's your country. If you're convinced the danger's genuine, I'm willing to abide by your judgment."

As the two talked, the police physician helped Lyons remove his jacket and sweatshirt. Lyons paid little attention. The doctor then pushed Lyons over the hood of Obilich's car and went to work with tweezers and antiseptic.

Obilich seemed happy for the few seconds' respite. It took no mindreader to see that he expected Lyons to make numerous demands and many arguments. Finally he said, "There are six in your party. We have no proof that the chess players are the only targets. I can have twelve men with your party at all times. I might spare more, but with a rapid-response team standing by, I think that should be more than sufficient."

Lyons had been hoping the opening offer would be lower. The more Yugoslav security surrounded him the less chance he'd have to spring the two Russians. He was caught in a bind. To demand less would appear suspicious.

"That sounds adequate. Thanks. Now I have another matter to discuss with you."

"Yes?"

"The squad leader, Vanessa, saved at least one life. We'd like to express our appreciation but would not want anyone thinking she was being bribed. What do you suggest?"

"As I understand it, you peeled your shoulder saving her skin. I think the balance sheet is equal. You want to tell me she did her job well?"

Lyons nodded.

"You do not mention the others."

"They died in the line of duty. I will not slight such men."

Obilich nodded thoughtfully, studying Lyons with narrowed eyes. "They were armed, Mr. Lyons. You were not. How is it you were the ones to survive?"

"They were gallant, but they lacked experience."

"Your point is made. The dead will be honored. And I will tell Sergeant Vanessa Aleska that you have requested she stay in charge of those entrusted with your safety."

"You're an understanding man, Colonel."

Obilich nodded slowly. "She is a good soldier. I hope I make it clear when I say that my understanding and your machinations should not reward her with an early death. Do I make myself clear?"

Just then the doctor finished taping Lyons's shoulder. Ironman rose and put on his ruined jacket.

"I don't trust you, either," he told Obilich. Then he turned and began running back to the hotel.

14

Wherever they went, Pescador, Lyons, Gadgets and Pol were each flanked by two men in army uniform. Lao and Harju each had one male and one female for constant companions. The entire party was both guarded and under surveillance at all times, even in bed and in the can. Sergeant Vanessa Aleska surpervised all three shifts of guards.

The soldiers' Zastava Model 70 automatics had been supplemented with Model 56 machine carbines made by the same Yugoslav manufacturer. The carbines were based on the German MP-40s. Two stun grenades hung from each soldier's belt. Vanessa carried a Skorpion slung over her shoulder, wire stock out and barrel down, ready to be swung up for quick firing. Four stun grenades hung by their pins from her web belt. This method of carrying grenades caused those around her some consternation.

Pescador, Harju and Lao seemed unruffled by the constant companionship. Pol and Gadgets had begun playing games with their guards. On the surface they seemed to be cracking from the strain. Actually they were testing alertness. The final day of the tournament was the time to round up the two Russians. But Able Team had been so closely watched that it had not yet managed to get word to them.

To everyone's surprise, Lyons seemed to be enjoying the close surveillance. It escaped no one's notice that he and Vanessa spent more time together than professional duty made necessary. On two occasions the guards assigned to Lyons were given extended lunch breaks while Vanessa attended to his safety.

The morning of the second last day, after the adjourned games were played, Blancanales invited Zhdanov to lunch. The old man laughed as he accepted the invitation.

It was not difficult to arrange a situation in which private conversation was possible. Neither the Yugoslav soldiers nor the KGB agents had any intention of letting the other side sit closer to the lunch meeting. Pol, at his most diplomatic, suggested that the protectors take tables near each exit. He and Zhdanov had lunch in the middle of a crowded restaurant. One Yugoslav and one KGB operative sat near the entrance, while the other pair had a table near the kitchen and were constantly ducking large trays of food.

Zhdanov opened the conversation. "I had a feeling we would be talking again. You must find it frustrating to your plans to have such zealous watch over your every movement."

Pol had the uncomfortable sensation that Zhdanov knew what he was going to say. So he said nothing, which Zhdanov seemed not to mind, for he continued talking without allowing a break for Politician to contribute comment.

"I told you that I would do nothing either to help or to hinder. I still find that the most reasonable stance to adopt. However, I forgot to include in my calculations that I'm easily bribed. I did not suspect this of myself until you told me about the computer you're using to train your chess players, and which you used to so readily defeat three strong players."

He poured more brandy sauce over his *palacinke*, an Eastern European dish resembling cheese blintzes. Pol decided he was doing well enough in the conversation without saying anything. So he quietly enjoyed the food and waited for the old man to continue.

"If my observation of the games played by Miss Harju and Mr. Pescador is correct, you also have some way of preparing a player for the style of his opponent."

Politician broke his silence. "Correct," he said.

Now Zhdanov was silent. Finally he said, "You're the most brilliant conversationalist I've ever met."

"My comments would have been superfluous."

"Exactly, Mr. Blancanales. Do you realize how few people are bright enough to understand when their comments are not needed?"

Pol smiled. "Thank you for the compliment."

"I think you understand people very well. So I will tell you something I have never told anyone else, not even my wife. I have always had a dream...no, that is not the word...a fantasy that I play a match game against myself for some sort of championship." Zhdanov's voice grew passionate, eager. "Did you know that in Russia we do not talk about playing chess against an opponent? We play chess with a partner, striving to win, but through that strife creating a chess game, a work of art. I should like once to see what kind of art I would create with myself as a partner. Would your computer allow me to play as if I were also the opponent?"

Politician ate slowly, methodically, considering the proposition. He asked, "Could you find us a copy of all your games? In algebraic notation?"

"That would be easy. Copies of my complete games are available in the stores. I'm sure several are in international notation."

"If I had a copy right away, I think Dr. Lao could have her computer ready for you by tomorrow morning. If you don't get an adjourned game today, I think it would be possible. But how would you explain it to your friends over there?"

With his short stature the ex-world champion looked meek. But his bellow of laughter was far from meek.

"I would simply tell them the truth and take two with me to assure my safety. They would be delighted."

"The truth being what?"

"That through striking up a friendship with you, I've had a chance to play chess against yet another American computer. They would not let me break that appointment. If I died, they'd prop me in front of the board for a chance to see the computer."

"Then I'll see what I can arrange."

"Not so fast, my young friend. What is your price?"

Politician thought for a long time.

"Come, do not keep an old man in suspense."

"There is no price. If I can arrange it, you're welcome to play the computer."

"Do not play sneaky games. You would not have a price, but what will the price be for the person you arrange things with?"

Politician smiled and shook his head. "If it goes through, there will be no price."

"Are you telling me you don't need my help?"

"As you've guessed, our guards make life difficult. It would be nice if you'd take a message to two of your players, as a favor. But that's what you'd be doing, a favor. If I can arrange a game with the computer, it will be arranged whether you're able to help us or not."

"Why?"

"Acts of friendship require no exchange, no bargains."

It was Zhdanov's turn to eat in silence as he mulled over the situation. Nothing more was said until the end of the meal. The Russian ordered two vodkas and had one set before Blancanales.

Picking up his drink, Zhdanov made a toast, "*Druka.* Friends."

Politician and Zhdanov emptied their glasses.

Pol stood up and offered his hand. Zhdanov grinned and said, "You shall have a copy of all my games within the hour."

THE FINAL DAY of the computer tournament dawned. Harju had established a sufficient lead to win the women's section regardless of the outcome of her final match. Pescador led the men's field by half a point over the Little General, but the computer was his final antogonist.

A win by the Little General would assure Binary Control Systems huge future growth. An extra room had been set up for the overflow crowd of spectators eager to watch the game between Pescador and the machine.

The previous two days had dissipated much of the tension caused by the attempt on the Americans' lives. Many of the participants at the chess tournament felt a warm bonhomie rising, such as is generated between warriors everywhere, no matter which side they battle for. The contestants were smiling at each other again.

Able Team, Harju and Pescador jogged through the old city for the first time since the shoot-out. With their retinue of protectors trailing, it looked less like a fitness regimen than like army maneuvers. Four of the guards rode motorcycles, but the rest of the Yugoslavs puffed along behind the Americans. To everyone's relief, Vanessa clipped the stun grenades to her belt in a more conventional manner for the duration of the run.

After breakfast Zhdanov showed up at the men's suite. He had two nervous KGB types in tow; one of them held a communicator with the Send button held down.

Lao greeted the Russian with a reserved but genuine warmth. They spoke as one scientist to another. It took ten seconds for the conversation to take off above the heads of everyone else in the room. It was impossible to tell she'd been up most of the night, feeding games into the optical scanner and further modifying the chess program.

Politician helped dissipate some of the KGB agents' growing hostility by serving them strong tea in the Russian style. Without saying anything, he drew three glasses of tea from a samovar and offered them on a tray. Each operative took a glass from the tray and set it down untasted. Only when Politician drank from the remaining glass did they smile and thank him.

No game in the tournament had been watched more closely than Zhdanov against the computer programmed to play in his style.

The ex-world champion began with the English opening. A series of subtle shifting of the opening patterns followed, until Zhdanov found himself transposed into play against the Caro-Kann defense, a favorite of his later years as champion. When he realized what the computer had done, he clapped his hands in glee like a child. Even the KGB operatives smiled.

The subtle strategies and tactics of the game eluded everyone in the room except Zhdanov and Pescador. Even Harju, an international master, frequently shook her head at her inability to fathom the finer points of play.

When the game was well under way, Lyons tapped his personal escort on the shoulder, and together they slipped from the room. Once they were in the hall, he pronounced Vanessa's name. A grinning soldier nodded and spoke into his communicator.

Vanessa met them in the lobby. "What you want, Carl?"

"I want to find someone and speak to him. I want to do this without endangering the lives of you and your men."

"Who is this? Why is he so dangerous?"

"A man with information. People will kill to keep us from getting the information."

Her high forehead under the blond bangs furrowed. "This is something for Colonel Obilich, is it not?"

"This might be something Colonel Obilich will not want to know."

"Who is this person?" Vanessa persisted.

Lyons shook his head. "A foreign journalist. I have no proof of anything more."

She frowned. She understood they could not pick up a foreign journalist on only Lyons's say-so. It would cost too much in precious tourist dollars.

"One moment," she told Lyons and walked to the manager's office. Lyons was sure she'd use the telephone there. She was too good a soldier not to report to her commanding officer. Or was she arranging for the proposed excursion?

She returned five minutes later.

"If we go calling, we should have more of us."

Lyons's gamble had paid off.

"Let's take Mr. Schwarz and his friends."

Smiling at Lyons's use of the word "friends," she took a communicator from her belt and issued some orders.

Two minutes later Gadgets emerged from the elevator, followed by the inevitable "friends."

"What's up?" he asked Lyons.

"We're going calling on a journalist—unofficially."

"A once bald, now yellow-haired journalist?"

"You got it?"

"Great. It's about time we found out what this is about. We still don't know why they're after Pescador and Harju."

"My nose says it has something to do with the computer," Lyons answered.

He described Cannibal Jones in his current disguise to Vanessa, who retreated once more to the manager's office. When she emerged, she had the needed information.

"The security officer tells me that the man you seek is registered as Charles Johnston. He's in the bar at this moment."

As Lyons, Schwarz and the five Yugoslavs went into the bar, Lyons said, "I want to talk to him alone. The rest of you run interference."

Gadgets nodded. Vanessa translated the orders for the other four soldiers. They split into three pairs, taking tables all around the one where Jones, in his blond wig, sat with the blond woman Lyons had last seen driving a truck. Another man was at the table: a drab man with a few strands of hair brushed sideways over his balding head was speaking forcefully to Jones. His name was Esenin, and he was a KGB agent, but Lyons didn't know this. But Lyons did recognize him as the out-of-place waiter, tending the water jugs at the computer tournament in California.

Lyons spotted Slaughter Smith and O. D. Yus at another table, drinking vodka and arguing quietly. The six-foot-six Feces Fatheringham was at a table in a corner, trying to overcome the language barrier and sell something to two amused Yugoslavs. Lyons would have been willing to bet it was forged shares in IBM, Fatheringham's favorite con.

Lyons watched the drab man leave Jones's table and walk out of the bar. The Ironman then strode over to Jones's table and casually sat down. Jones faced him inquisitively, regarding him with more curiosity than concern.

Lyons wasted no time on preliminaries. "Why are you trying to kill the Americans?"

"I don't think we've had the pleasure," Jones said. His Southern drawl was hopelessly overdone, and the inflections were wrong.

"We keep missing each other," Lyons answered. "I notice you're using a cane today. Nothing serious, I hope. I'd like you alive long enough to answer questions."

"Just a sprained ankle, Mr.—"

"I was hoping you'd stay around and let me treat it."

"Are you a doctor, Mr.—"

"No. My cures are more permanent. My name's Death."

"How dramatic."

Lyons shrugged. "You believed it when you ran like hell as my bullets smashed through the windshield. You'll believe again when the bullets smash through you."

"Are you sure you're not confusing me with someone else?"

"It doesn't matter."

"You're making threats. I think it matters whether or not you're making them to the right person." Jones glanced to Doris Drane to encourage her smile of approbation.

"It doesn't matter," Lyons repeated. "I'm delivering the message to you. So you're the one intended."

Jones laughed. "You really shouldn't go around threatening journalists. It leads to bad press."

"File your story early. That way your paper will get it."

"Why do you tell me this? Wouldn't it be easier simply to kill me?"

Lyons shook his head. "The Gun Team fighters were cowards in Vietnam; they're bigger cowards now. I figure it's more fun to play out the game. It'll also be fun to put buckshot in your ass as you run, like you did the other day."

"The police were—"

"Irrelevant to cowards with a long history of cowardice," Lyons finished for him.

Cannibal Jones no longer seemed amused. He let out a shrill whistle. The other three members of the Gun Team leaped from their chairs and came over to the table.

"This is the hotshot bodyguard. His mouth's too big," Cannibal told his men. "Take him out."

Fatheringham's face broke into an angelic grin. With his huge paws he grabbed Lyons by the shoulders, lifting him easily from his chair.

"You're going to be fun," Feces crowed.

Lyons slapped his cupped palms over the giant's ears. The concussion didn't knock Fatheringham over but it caused him to release Lyons.

Before any of the Gun Team could react, each found the barrel of a Zastava nestled lovingly against an ear. Each decided that the dispute was between Feces and Lyons and was really no one else's business.

The dispute was short-lived. Lyons shot a straight jab to the giant's gut. The blow would have killed a lesser man; it left Feces doubled up, lying on the floor, gasping for breath.

Lyons led his contingent from the battlefield.

"Do you want that man arrested for assault?" Vanessa asked.

Lyons shook his head.

"What did you find out?" she persisted.

"I think they are allies of the terrorists. If so, they'll come for me soon."

"Should I ask for reinforcements?"

"I wouldn't. Just make sure nothing happens to the chess masters."

15

When Lyons, Gadgets, Vanessa and the four guards returned to the suite on the tenth floor, Zhdanov's battle against the computer was well into the middle game. Politician met them at the door with a report.

"The board's too complicated for me to follow, but Billy says that the game will break any move now."

"That's not all that's going to break," Gadgets told his friend. "Ironman just tossed the gauntlet in Cannibal Jones's teeth."

"Who is a cannibal?" Vanessa asked.

"You going to tell her?" Gadgets asked Lyons. "She's gone along with you so far, and it's her troops who'll be hit."

"Not if I can help it."

"How can you prevent it, if you don't cooperate?"

"Shhh," hissed Harju, who was completely absorbed in the game.

"Let's talk in the bedroom," Pol said.

He and Lyons, Schwarz and Vanessa retired to the bedroom shared by Pol and Gadgets. Lyons made sure no one was too close to the door before he shut it and leaned against it.

"Okay, Carl, you tell me what you do. What am I into?" asked Vanessa.

Lyons turned his cold blue eyes on her. "They'll try to kill us, of course."

"Why would you want them to do that?"

"We can't have them at our back forever."

"You have something up your sleeve, but I will not allow you to do this thing. We keep maximum security in place."

"You're the boss," Lyons told her, "but this one's too big for you."

"We'll see who it's too big for," she stormed. "I'm going to phone for reinforcements." She slammed the door behind her. As soon as she was gone, Lyons turned to Gadgets. "This room clean?"

"I can't find any bugs, but I don't have a sweeper."

"That'll have to do. I want you to ride up and down on those two elevators until you're sure you can get behind either control panel in twenty seconds."

Gadgets grinned. "That'll be a challenge. I'll probably have to take the screws from the plate ahead of time."

Lyons shook his head. "That's cheating. We can't have any signs of tampering until the last minute."

Gadgets rolled his eyes but nodded.

"We have to get the chess players to go down before we do; it gives them the best odds for their survival."

"What's the idea?" Pol asked.

"Think. Jones is a tactician. Where do you hit the enemy?"

"At the pinch point," Gadgets answered. "The point where they're most strung out."

"That has to be between our rooms and the tournament hall on the main floor. Smith doesn't want to kill Yugoslavs, if he can avoid it. Where's the one place they can get us alone?"

"The soldiers follow us everywhere..." Gadgets began then paused. "The elevator! First Vanessa sends down half the guard to secure the main controls and the main floor, then they cram us onto the elevator. The rest of the guards follow us down in the next elevator. They'll hit us in the elevator!''

"That's what I'm counting on," said Lyons. "That means they'll have to post someone on this floor to let them know when we start down."

"I get the picture," Gadgets said. "Okay, I'll find a way into those panels."

The door opened, and Vanessa returned to the room. "The next shift of guards is coming on duty early. We're going to make sure they don't get at you."

Lyons nodded. "Just don't forget the chess players. They're the ones who matter."

"Are you telling me how to do my job?"

"If necessary."

Vanessa glared at Lyons, but she didn't allow his comments to bait her into an argument. Pol sighed. Ironman had lost another friend.

Gadgets went on a shopping trip. He returned with an old-fashioned twist drill, a screwdriver, a hack saw and a file. He sat down and sawed the blade from the screwdriver and filed at the shaft of the blade.

In his absence there had been a sudden increase of tension around the chessboard; Zhdanov had engaged in a series of rapid exchanges and emerged a pawn up. By the time Gadgets and the extra soldiers arrived, Zhdanov considered himself far enough ahead to allow the computer to resign. He immediately grasped Lao's hand.

"Congratulations, Dr. Lao. The program comes closer to international master strength than any before. I'm so happy to have had the chance to play against myself."

When Zhdanov left with his KGB shadows, Pol asked, "What did he mean, 'international master strength'? He's a grand master; it gave him problems."

Lao smiled wistfully. "He let it."

"I don't get it."

Pescador explained, "The computer is very strong tactically, but strategically not so hot. It's easy to beat if I play to its weakness; difficult if I play to its strength."

Politician suddenly caught on. "Then you didn't need to lose that first game against it."

Pescador shrugged. "Who's to say? I got too cocky and thought I'd knock it apart where it was strongest. I didn't manage. Zhdanov did."

"Hey," Harju said, "it's time to get down to the tourney. I hate arriving at the last minute."

"You two go ahead," Lyons said. "The rest of us will wait for Gadgets."

Vanessa drew upon her doubled forces. She sent half down to the dining room with the two chess players. She stayed with the other half to keep an eye on Able Team. Two minutes later Gadgets had the screwdriver shank filed to his liking and fitted to the twist drill. He rose with the drill in hand.

"Let's go," he said.

Six soldiers checked out the hall—there was only a blond maid, vacuuming—then rang for an elevator. Three minutes later Vanessa received two reports on her communicator; the elevator and the lobby were secure.

Three more soldiers left the suite and checked the hall then rang for an elevator. When it arrived, they checked it and held it as Vanessa, her grenades clanking, and the last three guards escorted Able Team from the suite to the elevator. The remaining soldiers would wait for the next elevator.

Able Team and Vanessa stepped into the elevator. Vanessa fitted her key to the instrument panel, making the elevator an express directly to the main floor. As its doors closed, a corporal on the tenth floor used a communicator to notify the guards in the lobby that their charges were on the way. But they never arrived.

The instant the elevator doors closed, Lyons held Vanessa out of the way as Gadgets sprang to the control panel and, using the twist drill, removed the screws.

"Let me go," Vanessa demanded.

"Our lives depend on what we do," Lyons told her. "Do not interfere."

"I demand—"

"They rigged it," Gadgets interrupted. "No matter which button is pushed we stop on six."

"Stop us on seven," Lyons ordered.

"What—" Vanessa began.

"A death trap. They're waiting for us on the sixth floor."

"I won't interfere," Vanessa said.

Lyons released her. She ran a hand through her hair; she seemed cooperative. Any fight from her might mean a fatal delay. But Lyons was satisfied that she wouldn't resist his plans.

The elevator doors slid open on the seventh floor, and Able Team and Vanessa ran for the stairs. Gadgets led the way down, taking the steps three at a time. The five moved so quickly that the door to the stairwell and the elevator door closed simultaneously. The elevator was continuing its journey to the sixth floor.

Gadgets paused by the door to the sixth floor, his hand on the knob, ready to yank it open. Ironman turned to Vanessa and grabbed two stun grenades from her belt, leaving the pins behind. He let them fly as Gadgets yanked open the door.

Ten feet down the hall, the four male members of the Gun Team watched as the elevator doors began to open; Feces Fatheringham was about to toss a fragmentation grenade through the opening doors. Lyons bracketed them with the stun grenades, then Gadgets and Pol both pressed against the fire door to the stairs, forcing it shut. The other three clasped their hands to their ears.

First there was the lighter boom of the shrapnel grenade used by the Gun Team, then the two thunderclaps of the stun grenades, whose shock waves battered the Gun Team. A moment after that Able Team closed in on its enemy.

A quick flurry of blows rendered the group more permanently unconscious. The Gun Team were quickly searched, their room keys, identification and hand weapons confiscated.

"Their rooms are on the fifth floor," Pol reported.

"Go," Lyons commanded.

Able Team galloped downstairs and made for the Gun Team's rooms. The keys opened four out of five doors in a row; one member of Able Team stepped inside each room. Vanessa went with Lyons.

"What is this—" she began.

Lyons, standing just inside the door, shook his head and put his finger to his lips. He was holding the knob so it wouldn't latch. His ear was against the panel.

In a moment they heard someone emerge from the stairwell and move straight to the door where Lyons stood.

Suddenly Lyons yanked open the door and said, "Come in, Doris."

The only female member of the Gun Team froze. She was still disguised as a hotel maid—the one who had been vacuuming on the tenth floor.

Unseen by Drane, Lao glided behind her. When Drane's hand darted into her large handbag, Lao chopped down on her shoulder. A large automatic clattered to the floor. Lao shoved Drane into the room. Following, Lao quickly took the missing hotel key from Drane's handbag and went to the one unlocked room.

"Who is she?" Vanessa demanded.

"A member of the same team of killers you saw upstairs. Her name's Doris Drane, and she'd rather kill you than talk to you."

"That little bit of fluff?"

"A lot of people thought that. They're all dead now. Looks can be deceiving." Lyons answered absentmindedly, most of his attention focused on Drane.

"What now?"

"Pat her down. Watch out especially for long pins and ice picks. Be careful but thorough."

Vanessa's hands slid down Drane's body, following every curve and crevice. Her garments were removed and examined. Having read Drane's dossier, Lyons expected hidden weapons, but he was astounded at what Vanessa's contour search unearthed: a derringer, a triangular-bladed stiletto and four sharp pins ranging from three to six inches long.

"Watch her carefully," Lyons told Vanessa.

He searched the room as thoroughly as Vanessa had searched Drane. As he finished, the rest of Able Team entered, laden with the spoils of their own searches.

The guns were unusual. The automatics were all like the one knocked out of Drane's hand: ugly, square boxes with barrels sticking out of the upper box. The subguns were also odd.

"Webbleys and Sten Mark 4As," Politician said. "They've got a contact in the British embassy."

"So it would seem," Lyons said. "Let's divide the ammo."

"What's the point?" Vanessa asked. "We will have to take them away from you again."

"Not this time," Lyons growled. "We have things to do." He turned to Politician. "Is the paperwork okay?"

"We've got it. Most of it was in their pockets."

"Let's go. Something stinks about this tournament. We stick in the two tournament rooms until this is over."

"I see your plan now," Vanessa said. "You think we will leave you armed in the tournament room rather than cause a disturbance. You might be right, but Colonel Obilich doesn't intend to give you the chance to try it.''

Sergeant Aleska pulled a small two-way radio from her uniform pocket and pressed the transmit button.

STEFAN BARAZOV, known in the terrorist world as the Shrew, had not survived fifteen years of bloodletting by trusting his fellow man. Especially, he didn't trust the KGB. He didn't trust them to honor their word unless it suited them. And he didn't trust them not to foul up. As far as Barazov could see, the KGB and the Americans were having a contest to see which side could blunder the most.

His mistrust of his KGB masters had long ago evolved into a standard working philosophy. His rules were few and simple but they kept him operating effectively when hundreds of other KGB pawns were either dead or rotting in Western jails.

Rule one: don't deliver the goods until paid.

Rule two: watch your back.

Rule three: cut all the nonessentials from a mission. The KGB and other intelligence organizations usually tripped up by trying to do too much at once. This plan was a prime example. Steal a computer. Kidnap only Russians. Make sure one Russian didn't survive. Do all this when it was sure the Yugoslavs would take the operation as a personal insult and do their best to have Barazov's scalp.

Rule four: don't use the KGB timetable. Inevitably there would be a leak and things would go wrong.

Abiding by his four rules, Barazov had considerably modified Esenin's plan. He would hit the tournament on the morning of the last day, not in the late afternoon when he was no longer sure where the computer or any of the players would be. He would take as many hostages as possible, especially Americans, as protection against the Yugoslavs. The United States was always good for a hefty ransom.

In keeping with this plan, he and thirty well-trained Bulgarians dressed in Yugoslav army uniforms arrived at the hotel in two stolen army trucks half an hour after the last games of the tournament had begun.

A driver and two guards stayed with each truck. The other twenty-four soldiers marched through the lobby to the tournament rooms without anyone questioning their presence.

The guards around Pescador and Harju knew of the trouble on the sixth floor and were not surprised at the arrival of further reinforcements. They had no idea that anything was amiss until the Bulgarian terrorists were close enough to cut them down.

It happened very fast.

Barazov rounded up all the Russian chess players, carefully weeding out the KGB operatives, the two Americans, and for safety, the three Yugoslav entrants in the tournament. The terrorists carried the computer in the middle of the group, keeping the hostages on the outside, and marched through the lobby to the waiting trucks. Their guns kept the procession quick and orderly. They were well on their way before anyone realized that it hadn't been Yugoslav soldiers that had made off with the chess players.

16

Furious and embarrassed, Colonel Obilich stormed into the hotel room where Able Team had just picked up the Gun Team's weapons.

"What do you know about what happened downstairs?" Obilich demanded.

"What *did* happen downstairs?" Lyons demanded, cold steel in his voice. The others froze, sensing that words might soon be replaced with bullets.

With calm authority, Obilich told him of the terrorist raid then asked, "What do you know about all this?"

Lyons turned to Vanessa. "You'd better tell your boss the rest of it."

Obilich raised an eybrow and received a terse report of the battle on the sixth floor. When she finished, Obilich turned back to Lyons.

"How did you know this attempt on your lives was going to take place?"

"I goaded them into it."

"Why?"

"I knew they'd separate us from our guards. We have business to attend to."

If Obilich was surprised by Lions's directness, he hid it well. "What business?"

"Let's change the subject for a moment. Have you thought how this will look?"

"I'm too busy trying to coordinate a search for those trucks to worry about politics. Suppose you tell me how you think it will look."

"Colonel, I'll repeat the facts; you consider their public relations value. Your troops herded the guards assigned to the American players onto a supposedly express elevator that stopped unexpectedly on a floor where a grenade was tossed into it. Just after that, a troop of soldiers wearing Yugoslav uniforms hauled away the Americans, the Russians, and to make it look good, the Yugoslavs. Of course, they took the computer."

"They did. How did you know?"

"It's the only thing that makes sense. Whoever set the Bulgarians loose inside a Communist bloc nation had to have a strong motive. The computer is the only answer. But we were talking public relations."

"I'm not a simpleton. I know that there will be much trouble, much of it for me. Yugoslavia will be blamed, and its international reputation will suffer. Western tourists will stay away, and Western bankers will refuse to renegotiate our loans. You're not throwing this in my face to win friends. What are you getting at?"

"Give us a chance to pull your nuts out of the fire. Only the KGB would want the computer that badly. If we can get the hostages and the computer back quickly, you get the glory, and the KGB gets the black eye."

"I fail to see why we should turn the matter over to you."

"It's our specialty. We do it best. Besides, you might be able to make it look like the Russians and the Americans having a dispute in your yard."

Obilich waved the last comment away. He was more interested in results. "Are you really the experts you claim to be?"

"We're still alive. Check with Brognola through the White House, but don't stand here prattling. There's work to be done."

Obilich stroked his chin. "That's blunt enough," he said in his clipped Oxford accent. "I'll take your word on your expertise. What's the price?"

"Our van, your help, and not too careful a scrutiny of our passports when we leave."

Obilich's face lit up. "Now it makes sense! I never quite trusted you. You were too good for the job you were doing.

"As you pointed out, I've little to lose. If you manage to return the chess players unharmed, we won't even count heads when you leave. If the KGB and its Bulgarian friends wish to soil our reputation, I care little how much rubs off back on them."

Obilich borrowed Vanessa's communicator and barked a series of orders. His voice and manner changed as he turned back to Able Team. He was now a field officer planning a campaign.

"I already have a good idea where the trucks will head, and spotters in place. The supposition that we're dealing with Bulgarian nationals limits their flight options."

Lyons nodded. Obilich continued, "Your expertise is appreciated. Warsaw nations have little experience with terrorism, other than hijackings. When a government eliminates the terrorists, no matter how many innocents are killed, the terrorists quickly learn their tactics don't pay."

"Yeah. Look how easily they're giving up in Afghanistan."

Obilich grimaced impatiently. "I was not giving you a political harangue. I want you to understand we don't have your type of experience. This time we cannot afford to have the foreign nationals harmed.

"Your van is on the way. Sergeant Aleksa and I will accompany you to act as liaison with army and police. As soon as we have any indication which direction to go, we'll move. Does that suit you?''

Lyons gestured to Doris Drane. ''What happens to her and the four you picked up upstairs?''

Obilich paused. ''They're a problem. Without your testimony, a trial would be touchy. We're not fond of the story that will come out.''

Lyons met Drane's hostile glare directly as he said, ''Deport them for the illegal arms found in their rooms. We'll take care of them later.''

Obilich nodded. ''Let's move downstairs. We want to be ready to move the instant we get word.''

An hour later the two trucks were located.

''They're headed for the Bulgarian border,'' Obilich reported. ''I suppose the moment they see a roadblock they'll simply hold guns to the heads of the hostages and keep going. I suppose all we can do is stop them and negotiate.''

''We can do a hell of a lot more,'' Lyons snapped. ''Show me their position and heading on a map.''

''I'll do that on the way to the airport. We have at least one advantage—speed.''

Vanessa drove Able Team's van while the others bent over Obilich's map.

''This is what we want,'' Lyons snapped. ''Those trucks aren't to see a trace of police or army. Plaster the area with army dressed as road workers. I want accidents and road work to slow up those Bulgarians. Can you do that?''

For an answer, Obilich picked up his communicator. Gadgets grabbed his wrist.

''What's the range of that thing?''

''In the city? Damn little.''

''Okay. Just make sure that the instructions are relayed by telephone. I'll bet the Bulgarians are monitoring your frequencies.''

Obilich flushed and put down the communicator. "I'll take care of everything by telephone. Thank you for the reminder. What will you need in the way of arms? How much tear gas?"

Lyons shook his head. "No tear gas. One whiff and the terrorists will kill their prisoners. Instead we'll need army uniforms."

This time Obilich used the communicator.

"Your uniforms will arrive at the airport shortly after we do."

When they arrived at the airport, Vanessa drove through the gate and straight onto the tarmac. A MIL MI-10 was waiting for them, the 115-foot rotors slowly turning over. The paratroop sergeant parked near the massive helicopter as ground crew began buckling the van to the sky crane.

Obilich jumped out of the van, commandeered the first ground vehicle he found and sped off in search of a telephone.

An emergency response police van came screaming up to them, with battle fatigues for all of them. The uniforms bore the insignia of colonel. An army offical told them that "Colonel Obilich says it is best you be colonels also. Colonels do not answer questions." He laughed as if he'd just told the funniest joke he knew.

Fifteen minutes after their arrival at the military airport, Able Team was skyborne, still in their van, which was suspended beneath the helicopter.

"Hey, Pol," Gadgets jibed. "This is the smoothest driving you've done for a long time."

Pol gave him a tired smile. "I hope those nylon straps hold. I don't think the shocks could take the jolt."

"How long will it take this bird to catch up to the Bulgarians?" Lyons demanded.

Obilich said, "Unfortunately, this helicopter slurps petrol faster than a commissar downs vodka. By stretching our reserves to the limit, we'll be able to set the van down in a paved area to the west of Pristina. That should put us no more than fifteen minutes behind the trucks. But we've got all the necessary communication in place to allow us to use main roads to get in front of the trucks.''

Nothing more was said for the rest of the flight. The Able Team members removed their weapons from the various caches and checked them carefully. All the communicators were checked and two given to Obilich. These alone would be guaranteed safe from Bulgarian eavesdropping. When everything was prepared, the warriors made themselves as comfortable as possible.

Obilich looked from one to another of the four and then at his sergeant. "If I ever doubted their credentials before," he told her quietly, "I do not now. Such battle preparedness is not given to common soldiers such as you and I."

She nodded. She was ready, willing to do battle. She knew she was capable. But she could only marvel at these four who relaxed before battle, simply because that was what was required.

The giant helicopter descended to a paved area barely large enough for the monster. Farm machinery had been hauled off the paved area to make space. A fuel truck was standing by to fill the chopper's huge tanks for the return flight.

Politician sat in the driver's seat of the van, and Obilich was beside him to navigate and clear them through roadblocks. Vanessa sat behind Politician, ready to take the wheel if necessary. Lyons and Lao sat near the wide side door; Lyons kept a map spread on his lap. Gadgets slouched in the seat behind Obilich.

The moment the van touched down, half a dozen men in combat fatigues rushed up to unhook the vehicle. Two dispatch riders and a captain lined up to talk to Colonel Obilich. Two motorcycle police pulled in front of the van, ready to give escort.

Obilich accepted some dispatches from a courier, gave him one of Gadgets's communicators and a spate of rapid-fire orders. The soldier saluted, tucked the radio into his pouch and ran for his motorcycle.

It was the captain's turn, but he was waved to one side. Obilich took a verbal report from the other dispatch rider and sent the other communicator with him. Only then did he turn his attention to the captain for a briefing.

After the captain left, Obilich filled in Able Team. "We have rerouted the trucks. They're struggling over nearly impassable roads. The motorcycles will escort us along the main highway to a point where we can intercept. They wish to know how fast you can drive this van and still maintain safe control."

"What sort of road?" Politician asked.

"Excellent highway, most of the way."

Pol quickly converted 150 miles per hour into kilometers. "If they can handle 250, so can we."

"You jest, perhaps?"

Politician shook his head. He'd floored the van before they left the States. It would do 170 flat out, but the fuel consumption was too high. The motor was the best technology Detroit could give him.

When the dispatch riders were given the figures, they smirked. They seemed to think that some crazy officer didn't know how fast an American van would go. They took off with a roar, determined to do the required speed and leave the van far behind.

The motorcycles' sirens cleared traffic to the shoulder on the nearly deserted roads.

When they accelerated, the 650cc machines easily left the van behind, but on the long curves and smooth stretches of the highway, the van gained easily on them.

As they devoured the highway, Obilich and Lyons consulted. Lyons plunked his finger down on the map so hard his fingernail cut through.

"Right here. I want them rerouted along the river. I also want them separated."

"They'll never believe that any detour would take them along that old river road," Obilich objected.

"Crash some trucks where they can see them. Block the road with the wrecks. They'll have to believe it."

Obilich nodded. "We'll try it. One of those communicators left five minutes before we did. I'll get a report as soon as it arrives. I'll try to arrange it."

"See if you can also arrange some scuba gear—flippers, tanks and face masks—for Ti and myself."

Obilich nodded.

Lyons turned back to the map, pointing at a stretch of road that ran alongside the river. "Here's where we're going to make contact."

Obilich didn't look convinced. "What can you do in such a narrow zone?"

Lyons grinned. "Watch."

Twenty-eight minutes later a motorcycle rider reached them with the scuba gear, and then the motorcycle police left them at a turnoff onto a secondary road. Obilich was busy with the communicator, issuing commands and getting reports, but he kept them enroute.

Seventeen minutes later, he reported, "We are now ahead of the trucks by about four minutes."

Lyons stared out the windshield. "Fast," he told Pol. "We need another two minutes."

The van lurched and bumped over the dirt roads.

Five minutes later Lyons yelled, "This is it. Pol, Gadgets, this is your best spot. Everyone out, but Lao and I."

There was a farm building of unfinished planks near the road, causing a blind turn. Pol, Gadgets and the two Yugoslavs scrambled out. Lao slid into the front and threw the van into gear. Pol watched the van leap down the road like a lame rabbit.

"You and the colonel taking the first truck?" Gadgets asked.

Pol nodded.

"Okay. When you spot the van, go for it."

Gadgets and Vanessa hurried up the road to meet the trucks they could already hear laboring toward them. Pol and Obilich disappeared around the blind corner.

"Okay, sergeant, do your stuff," Gadgets said. "That first truck has to be willing to stop and speak to our two colonels up there."

She nodded and flagged the oncoming army truck. The driver stuck his head out the window. Clearly edgy. "What is this, sergeant?"

"We'll be setting up roadblocks here. Better get your pass from Colonel Luska."

"Who?"

"Just around the bend. The colonel will give you a pass that should see you through."

The driver smiled. "What's happening?"

"Some excitement in Dubrovnik," Vanessa told him.

"Sounds like Russian drivel to me."

Grinning at the easy out being offered, the driver slowly wheeled his truck around the blind corner.

Seeing the first truck pass, the second driver stopped his vehicle.

"What's happening?"

"The next side road will take you to the highway. You shouldn't have any trouble from there," Vanessa said.

The driver was instantly suspicious. "They have a sergeant and a colonel waiting to tell us that?"

Vanessa leaped onto the runningboard. "I want your serial number, soldier."

The terrorist riding shotgun was so interested in the fiery blond sergeant that he neglected to keep an eye on the bored-looking colonel. It was a fatal error. Gadgets, in a colonel's uniform, leaped onto the runningboard and slammed his fist into the man's temple. He was unconscious before he knew he'd been hit. Gadgets opened the passenger door and let the body tumble out.

Alarmed, the Bulgarian driver turned toward Gadgets. His momentary inattention of Vanessa allowed her to snake an arm around his neck. While he struggled, Gadgets's Mark II made its mark in his heart.

Vanessa kicked the body free, slid into the seat and put the truck in gear.

"The Bulgarians in back probably know their truck's been hijacked," Vanessa said as she negotiated the tight curve.

"They'll stay down until the truck's clear of the army people in the road. After that, we'll just have to keep them too busy hanging on to sneak a peek."

She grinned. "That should be fun." She smoothly shifted up a gear and put the pedal to the floor.

Policitician and Obilich had an even easier time of it. Obilich stopped the first truck with a query about supplying a pass. Politician used his silenced 93-R to punctuate Obilich's sentences. Two shots from two feet away into two heads furnished the hoped-for passes—straight to hell. The bodies were unceremoniously dumped. Obilich had the truck rolling within ten seconds—so fast that probably none of the Bulgarian soldier-terrorists in back had even noticed the change.

"The other truck is moving like hell," Obilich observed.

"Probably keeping the passengers rattled. We'd better do the same."

Obilich sweated as he maintained the truck on the rough and narrow road, but he gamely slammed down the accelerator. From the back came bellows of rage, barely audible over the roar of the laboring engine.

Someone was banging on the back of the cab. Gadgets and Obilich ignored it. Finally Obilich let up slightly on the accelator.

"There it is!" he shouted.

Able Team's van was parked just off the road on the right. On the left was the river. Pulling hard on the wheel, Obilich maneuvered the truck down the bank and into the river. It didn't stop until it was entirely submerged.

17

Vanessa saw the truck ahead ride into the cold clear water of the northern branch of the Beli Drim River. She floored the accelerator and drove her truck down the steep limestone bank and into the water as well. The four-ton vehicle settled five feet from the first truck, tilted toward the driver's side.

Gadgets braced his foot against the steering column and pushed his door up and open. He reached down and pulled Vanessa upward. She scrambled along his body and out the open door, where she anchored herself with one hand and helped Gadgets out with the other.

When they surfaced, Gadgets pushed her toward the near bank. Then he pulled a strong crawl stroke straight across the river and let the current carry him. He reached the far bank a hundred feet downstream from the trucks.

Thirty feet away, Gadgets saw Lyons point out a cache of arms to Obilich. When the colonel moved toward the arms, Lyons bit down on the mouthpiece of his scuba gear and vanished into the fast-flowing river. Gadgets headed toward Obilich on the double.

By the time he reached the cache, Obilich had already slung his web belt on and now helped Gadgets into his. Both fastened their belts quickly. Gadgets was armed with both his own Ingram and Lyons's Konzak assault shotgun. Spare clips festooned the belt, making Gadgets look like a soggy overdecorated Christmas tree. Obilich had his Skorpion and plenty of extra clips.

The heads of both terrorists and captives had appeared in the dark blue river. Lao was already underwater somewhere. On the opposite bank, flitting among the scrubby trees clinging to a limestone cut, Vanessa and Politician armed themselves from a similar cache of weapons that had been left by Lao. Politician was shaking the water from the barrel of his 93-R. Vanessa, gripping her Model 70, was already wading back into the water, extending her hand to a struggling man whom she identified as one of the Russian chess players.

Obilich saw a man in a Yugoslav army uniform swimming downriver, away from the trucks. He stood with the Skorpion extended at arm's length. A short burst from the Czech subgun blasted the swimmer's head off.

Lao, wearing mask, tanks and large flippers, kicked her way up against the current into the back of the first truck. Visibility was not good under the canvas flap, but it took her only forty seconds to make sure everyone had escaped. There was nothing left in the truck, no bodies or packages. She kicked out into the river.

In the back of the second truck Lyons found two bodies and several weapons. A quick pat-down of the bodies told him one was in uniform. He left it there. The other he dragged to the nearest bank as quickly as possible. Two of the rescued chess players took the limp form, pumped the water from his lungs and started artificial respiration. Lyons sank back into the river.

Politician extended his hand to Harju, who swam to shore like an Olympic champion. Behind her a man in an army uniform swam almost as strongly. As Pol pulled Harju to the bank with one hand, with his other he fired his Beretta at the man in the water. At the same time there was a cry for help from midstream. It came from a Russian player who was unable to swim. He was struggling and spluttering. Harju dived back into the water and swam to the panic-stricken man.

Gadgets waded into the river up to his waist. The terrorists were realizing that they weren't victims of a traffic accident. There was a flurry to grab hostages as protection against the avengers on the banks. One prisoner almost made the shore when he was overtaken by a Bulgarian terrorist. Gadgets slammed the butt of his MAC-10 into the side of the terrorist's neck. Leaving the terrorist to float downstream facedown, Gadgets helped a coughing Yugoslav chess master to the rocky bank.

Holding a long-bladed diver's knife, Lyons swam up under each struggling figure and felt for a uniform. When he felt the distinctive cloth and buttons of the Yugoslav military, he made the killing slash. Dead, uniformed bodies were floating along the river.

Harju's long golden hair streamed behind her as she swam to the aid of the drowning Russian. It was too tempting a target for a Bulgarian terrorist in need of a hostage. He grabbed her hair and wound it around his hand. At the same time another killer with the same idea grabbed her legs. Harju was pulled under.

A small form inserted itself in the tangle of bodies. This figure was woman-shaped and had air tanks strapped to her back. Arms wrapped themselves around the head and jaw of the first attacker. Small legs anchored themselves around his waist. There was a convulsive heave. Underwater, the sound of a neck bone snapping seemed especially loud.

While Harju untangled her hair from the dead man's hand, Lao thrust herself at the second terrorist, her hands outstretched. She jammed two fingers into the eyes of the Bulgarian. He released Harju and grabbed Lao's hands. Lao let him grab then doubled into a ball and thrust her feet into his stomach. The force knocked the air from his lungs.

He tried releasing her wrists, but the small hands caught his with crushing strength. He scarcely noticed the pain, since he was inhaling river water. Lao released the terrorist to drown. She looked for Harju, who had already resumed her rescue mission.

Lyons and Lao stayed underwater, attacking from underneath. Believing their opposition was on the banks, the surviving terrorists struggled to find a hostage, unaware of the proximity of Death.

Gadgets was surprised when someone emerged from the water beside him: Pescador. To avoid being spotted by the Bulgarian hoodlums, he had swum away from the trucks underwater. Both Pescador and Gadgets whirled toward each other then grinned with recognition.

Then Gadgets turned his attention back to the river where he had a clear head shot at a terrorist who was clutching a hostage. Pescador moved down the bank to help a chess player from the water.

One of the surviving terrorists spotted Lyons and yelled a warning. Two terrorists immediately dived to find they were directly over the underwater intruder. One grabbed Lyons's wrist on the hand holding the knife as the other wrenched the air-supply mouthpiece from between Lyons's teeth.

He doubled up and twisted. The swimming Bulgarians had no anchor to allow them to resist the contortions of Ironman's powerful body. His long legs closed around the neck of the man who held his wrist.

The other attacker hammered Lyons in the solar plexus to force him to expel the small amount of air in his lungs. The water weakened the blows; Ironman simply tightened his abdominal muscles and ignored the flailing fists.

Lyons slowly straightened his legs as the other goon lost his grip on his wrist. Lyons straightened, and the Bulgarian, caught by the neck, trailed behind him.

The attacker hammering Lyons's gut saw the knife arcing toward his exposed ribs. He rolled and caught Ironman's hand in both of his. Ironman's free hand struck the man between the ribs, accomplishing with a well-placed thumb to the ribs what the other's punches could not do. The victim explosively exhaled, gulped water and made for the surface. Lyons's blade flashed, cutting the main artery behind the Bulgarian's right knee. He broke surface, leaving a trail of spurting red in the water behind him. Lyons forgot him. By the time he cleared his lungs of water, he'd be too weak to swim to shore.

Calmly blasting the mouthpiece clear of water, Lyons exhaled and popped it back into his mouth. By the time he'd drawn a few deep breaths, the man clasped between his legs was dead.

The battle of the river moved downstream to a platoon of genuine Yugoslav troops. They had chosen a shallow to form a human chain across the surging current. From there they dragged the bodies from the water and lay them on the bank.

As the Able Team warriors moved downstream, pulling out chess players and eliminating terrorists, they reached this line of infantry. Lyons and Lao waded out of the water, and Lyons loudly demanded an immediate head count. The platoon sergeant understood English and was about to give him the news when Obilich shook his head.

He called to Lyons, "The news is not bad, but we had better discuss things before numbers are mentioned."

Puzzled, still wearing his flippers and tank, Lyons plodded over to Obilich.

"What is it?"

Obilich seized his hand and pumped it. "First, I must congratulate you on your brilliant strategy. The jaunt into the river appeared so much like an accident that the terrorists did not attempt to kill their hostages until it was too late.

"I feel I owe you something. We could not have had such an excellent result without your planning and execution. So I had the victims taken immediately to farmhouses where they are being given hot tea and being dried off. Of course, being host to so many would be a strain on only one or two farmers; so each victim is being guarded at a separate location."

"What's this to do with a head count?"

"The Russian and Yugoslav players are more ignorant of the results than yourself. I congratulate you again. Unofficially, you have a perfect score: all victims alive, all kidnappers dead."

"Unofficially?"

"Officially, I cannot find even one of the Russian players. They may have been swept downstream before I managed to get the troops in place."

Lyons smiled nervously.

"What about the computer?"

"A crate was retrieved from the river near one of the trucks. There it is."

Lyons removed his flippers and walked barefoot to a wooden box, 2 x 2-1/2 x 3 feet, made of inch-thick boards. He grabbed a board and pulled. It snapped with a report like a high-powered rifle. He did it again. In two seconds all four boards in the front of the crate were removed.

Lyons used his knife to lever the boards away, quickly prying open the box as the Yugoslav soldiers watched silently.

Lyons pulled away a layer of plastic and stood looking at a pile of computer parts.

"Lao," he roared.

Lao strolled up, toweling her short hair.

"Could this junk have been the Little General?"

Lao dropped the towel, peered into the box and picked up a circuit board. She gave it a half-second inspection and tossed it to one side. She then dipped her hand into the box to inspect other parts. They littered the riverbank as Lao dipped her hands alternately into the fractured crate, glanced at each find then tossed it away.

Two minutes later she looked up from the center of a circle of rubble and said, "No."

"What do you mean 'No'?" Obilich demanded.

"I've used the microprocessor from Little General. There isn't one here." Lao gestured at the parts strewn around her. "Garbage." She picked up the towel and walked away, drying her hair.

"The computer must still be in one of the trucks," Obilich insisted.

"Ask."

The SDB colonel stared at Lyons. "Ask who?"

"The chess players. They'll know if the computer was there."

Obilich barked a rapid series of orders. Half the troops scurried away.

Politician pulled up with the van, allowing the Able Team warriors to change into their own dry clothes. Each put on a flak jacket and strapped on a concealed handgun. Obilich and Vanessa turned their backs and went in search of dry uniforms for themselves.

"Colonel," Lyons called after him. "Has the MI-10 taken off yet?"

"I suspect so. Why?"

"We're going to need it."

Obilich signaled a soldier over to him. The soldier carried an East bloc communications outfit, sixty pounds of radio gear and batteries. It took several minutes to convince the others that they could break radio silence and to get patched through to the temporary landing site.

Obilich called to Lyons, "The pilot went for a long lunch while the helicopter was being fueled. It's warming up now."

"Keep it hot and set up the trip back."

Obilich shrugged. "I don't see your reasoning, but seeing he's still there, we may as well go back that way." He turned back to the communications gear.

The soldiers started filtering back from the surrounding farmhouses. Each one answered the colonel's raised brows with a shake of the head or a loud "No, sir." The chess computer had not been in the truck to begin with.

"I need some more favors," Lyons told Obilich.

"I'll be with you as soon as I change."

Lyons shook his head. "Stay here and look for the two missing bodies. It'll make your story better. You don't want to know what we're doing."

"But I do. I'll send Sergeant Aleska back with you. She might be able to keep you out of trouble, but I doubt it."

Lyons walked over to the colonel and proffered his hand. "It's good to work with a pro."

"Isn't it, though?" Obilich replied. "I guess we won't meet again. Sergeant Aleska will bring two unidentified hitchhikers back with her."

Lyons raised a brow.

Obilich gave him a faint smile. "Once I knew *why* you were here, the *who* was easy—too easy. Watch your step."

The two men shook hands.

Lyons turned to Able Team. "Don't stand around. We have work to do."

18

The trip back to Dubrovnik was only slightly less hectic than the trip out. It took less time because there was no need to detour the terrorists' trucks. But with the huge helicopter carrying Able Team's van, it took longer than conventional air travel.

The van was even more crowded. Obilich wasn't with them; Sergeant Aleska sat in his place, clutching hastily written orders that indicated she was acting on the colonel's behalf. In the back, along with Harju and Pescador, Lao, Pol and Gadgets, sat Tsigal Manolis and Igor Kubasov, dressed like Yugoslav farmers. Both were recently of Russia but were about to become Americans. All four chess players grinned. For the members of Able Team, there was still work to be done. They would grin when the assignment was over.

"We go to the plane now, yes?" Manolis asked.

"We go to war now," Lyons replied.

The grins were replaced by questioning looks. Lyons ignored them and turned to Vanessa.

"Can you arrange for our four friends to be cared for secretly, near the airport?"

"This computer matters so much?"

"I don't give a damn what happens to the computer, but the KGB aren't going to have it," Lyons growled.

Vanessa laughed. "I knew you would say words like that. Yes, I will find a spot both secret and safe for our friends."

"Can you have someone watched?"

Vanessa waved the hastily scrawled authorization Obilich had given her. "With this I can have someone shot."

"Watched would be better. We'll shoot him after he leads us to the computer. I'm willing to bet he's staying at the same hotel we are, but he may be somewhere else." Lyons described the waiter he'd first noticed at the computer chess tournament in California—and again at Cannibal Jones's table in Dubrovnik. His name was Mr. Esenin. "Make sure he doesn't know he's watched. I'll bet he's sharp," Lyons finished.

"I think we can manage. Is there anything else?"

"Telephone for me. Then food," Lyons commanded. It was late afternoon. Able Team and Vanessa had missed lunch.

Vanessa busied herself with Able Team's radio. Reception was excellent in spite of the van's aerial being so close to the MI-10's engines.

When the helicopter finally returned to the military field in Dubrovnik, the van was unfastened; Vanessa had Pol drive it to the edge of the field. They waited there for ten minutes.

A military truck, similar to the two they'd driven into the river, pulled up beside Able Team's van. A captain climbed down from the cab. Vanessa strode over and saluted. They conferred. He examined the note from Obilich and handed it back to her, shaking his head in puzzlement.

After that, Able Team was fitted with fresh uniforms from the back of the truck. They dressed quickly, putting the military fatigues on over their flak jackets.

Lao was the major problem. The smallest jacket fit well, although fractionally tight across the shoulders and chest. The truck driver, an equivalent of quartermaster, solved the problem of her pants by hacking off the excess leg length with a knife. She wouldn't pass muster alone, but in the middle of a group would probably get away with it.

She did deep knee bends and stretches before she accepted the clothes. Finding that nothing restricted her free movement, she nodded.

This time none of the Able Team warriors held officer's rank. They appeared to be a squad under Sergeant Aleska's command.

The four chess masters were equipped with the fatigues of new recruits.

Vanessa explained, "There is KGB throughout the armed forces, and SDB. But no one will pay attention to new recruits. Captain Nusic will see to their safety."

It took time to convince the Russians they were being turned over to the Yugoslav army only for their own safety. The sight of the American chess players accepting the same role finally convinced them.

When the chess players had donned their new uniforms, Vanessa herded Able Team back into the van as if it were genuinely her squad.

"Follow the truck," she ordered Politician.

They drove deeper into the base. The first stop allowed Ironman access to a military telephone; his call to the American Air Base in Greece went through promptly.

The air force had an old C-130 Hercules standing by in Greece to pick up Able Team and its van. Ostensibly it would make a scheduled delivery of medicines to the civilian airfield near Dubrovnik. The tricky part was to get the van into the Hercules the moment the goods were unloaded. Lyons glanced at his watch. His call had put things in motion. He had four hours and forty minutes to make the connection.

The next stop was the mess, where the Able Team fighters joined the first supper shift. They might have blended in if they hadn't gone through the line twice. Ironman was just finishing his third tray load, when a soldier hurried over and spoke in Vanessa's ear.

"The man you wanted watched has departed the hotel," she told Lyons.

Within seconds they were in the van and on their way. Holding an Able Team communicator which Gadgets had tuned to one of the SDB frequencies, Vanessa kept herself informed in Esenin's movements and told Pol how to set his course.

"He seems to be headed for the Soviet consulate," she said.

"Can we get there before he does?" Gadgets asked.

"Perhaps, but I'm not certain that's where he's heading."

"Try it."

Pol floored the van; the pace of driving changed from fast to hectic while Gadgets rummaged through his electronic gear.

"We'll make it. He's doubling back to see if he has a tail," Vanessa reported.

"He spotted them?" Lyons demanded.

"I doubt it. You told me to get the best; I have our best. My guess is that it's standard routine." She turned back to Politican. "Pull over to the curb. The consulate is just around the corner."

The van screeched to a halt. Gadgets jumped out, ran to the corner and began to act as if he were staggeringly drunk. He did not meander all over the sidewalk in a comic parody of drunkeness. Instead he paused every few paces to pull himself erect and plan the next few paces. Just as it seemed he was going to stagger, he would pause again and seem to concentrate. It was a subtle act, more convincing than staggering would ever be.

The Soviet guards in front of the consulate watched in amused contempt as the Yugoslav private tried vainly to hide his drunkenness.

When the soldier almost reached the gate, he stood, not quite swaying, apparently fighting off an attack of nausea.

One guard was about to say something when a meek-looking man detoured past the soldier and turned toward the gate.

A guard spoke to the newcomer in Serbo-Croatian. The newcomer snapped back in Russian, and the guards stiffened. The drunk fell straight into the man as he was about to step past the guards, and he slid his hands along his trench coat. Then the two separated, and the drunken man fell.

Once the newcomer had entered the consulate, the guards picked up the drunk and told him to clear out. Gadgets didn't understand a word they said, but resumed his slow unsteady pace down the block. When he was out of sight of the Russians, he straightened up and jogged a long detour back to the van.

"I've just ruined the reputation of the Yugoslav army," Gadgets told Vanessa as he climbed back into the van.

"I had reports," she answered in a stiff voice. "The Soviet army has the largest rate of alcoholism in the world. You have delighted them in showing them a drunken member of our forces. Why?"

For an answer, Gadgets took her communicator and returned it. Voices in Russian crackled forth.

"Not very clear."

"It's small and on the back of his coat, but we can follow it," Gadgets answered as he set up his directional antennas.

"What did you do?" asked Vanessa.

"I planted a bug on the very man your men have been watching for us," said Gadgets.

Seventeen minutes later, two Zil limousines left the Russian compound.

"My men say the man we follow is not in the cars."

"He is, though," Gadgets replied as he adjusted his directional tuner. "He must have ducked to throw off anyone watching for him."

Vanessa snapped orders into her communicator, and Pol pulled away slowly from the curb.

"The buildings are mostly stone. With so little metal to block the signal, we can give him a long tether," Gadgets told Pol; Pol nodded and drove slowly past the consulate. Lyons and Lao picked up their weapons.

Vanessa looked up from the communicator. "Much damn. Our men let the cars go through. Now they cannot catch up without being noticed."

"They've done their job," Lyons told her. "Tell them to go home."

"Please explain to me what we do," Vanessa asked.

"You must have figured it out by now?"

"The man we follow must be of the Komitet Gosudarstvennoi Bezopasnosti, but why do we follow the KGB?"

"Who else would be picking up the computer from the Bulgarians?"

Vanessa seemed surprised, and a question seemed to form itself on her lips, but it remained unspoken.

Lyons let her ponder the situation and raised his voice to brief the entire team. "We're not going to have much time to get in and get out. We don't know how many Bulgarians will be at the meeting. So don't try to capture the computer; just make sure the Russians don't get it."

"I'm not sure if this is something I should be helping," Vanessa said.

Lao said, "What does your heart say?"

Vanessa grinned. "We do."

Ten minutes later they were staring at a three-storey limestone house with a red tile roof. Outside, two Soviet Zil limousines were parked; their six male passengers had gone inside.

"What sort of place is that?" Lyons demanded.

"It's a fifteenth-century villa. We rent these places to tourists."

"Smooth," Politician said. "Our Bulgarian rents a villa for himself and his men then checks into the hotel where he can keep an eye on things. Then when they made the raid, he simply put the computer in the trunk of a car and drove here while we chased the two army trucks all over hell's half-acre."

"How thick are the walls?" Lyons asked.

"In an old house like that? Probably no more than thirty to fifty centimeters," Vanessa answered.

"A foot to twenty inches," Gadgets translated. "We're not going to blast through those walls with anything that won't shake down the entire neighborhood."

"Those small window casements are ideal for a firefight," Pol commented. "Ten men could hold off a battalion."

"Some of our Russian friends are returning," Pol noted as four Russians walked back to their cars.

The five piled out of the van, which was stationed a few doors down, leaving behind their weapons except for silenced handguns.

"When I shout, single file, double time," Vanessa said.

Lyons nodded. "As good a plan as any."

Vanessa barked orders in one of her native languages, and Able Team jumped to obey. They ran single file along the middle of the road, apparently unarmed, ignoring the staring Russians who were sitting in twos in the parked cars.

It was dusk. The Russians didn't notice the silenced hand weapons until it was too late. They tried to bring up the subguns from their laps, but the silenced guns coughed before careless hands could reach the triggers. With four accurate head shots in one second, Able Team hastened to drag the Russians to the side of the van and put on their clothes.

Lyons looked at the corpses and grunted with disgust. "Must be clerks conscripted by our friendly traveling KGB agent. No way these are field men."

Both Russians from one of the cars were small men. The two in the other car were larger but overweight. There was no way Lyons could wear any of their suits.

Lyons issued his battle orders while the other four changed clothes. "I'll start some fireworks to hurry the transaction. The Russians will come tearing out and into the cars before they notice the substitution. We're betting they'll have the computer with them."

"If they don't?" Vanessa asked as she tossed her fatigues into the van.

"Then at least we'll have divided their firepower."

Lao and Vanessa unselfconsciously put on the blue serge of the smaller men. Lao had short hair about the right color for the driver, so she took his place. Vanessa sat in the back with her hair hidden under the Russian's battered hat.

Politician took the wheel of the other Zil; Gadgets clambered into the back. All four kept their shoulder-harnessed handguns but couldn't risk taking more firepower into the limousines where it might be noticed.

Ironman took Politician's M-203/M-16 combo and a bandoleer of HE grenades and moved quietly around a neighboring house until he could see the back of the villa the Bulgarians were using as a safehouse. Two sentries were marching back and forth, assault rifles at the ready.

He plucked eight grenades for the M-203 grenade launcher from the bandoleer and placed them where he could quickly put his hand on them. Then he lined up the sights of the M-16 on the first sentry.

Two quick figure eights of .223 tumblers took care of the guards. Then Lyons snatched one grenade, rammed it home and lined up on the left third-floor window. He arced it through the window and slammed home the next grenade.

As the grenades soared, Lyons reloaded. Each grenade crashed into a different room. Inside the house shouts and cries of terror followed the explosions. Someone on the ground floor managed to sweep autofire toward Lyons, but the firing ceased abruptly when the second grenade hit, and the AK arced through the air with the terrorist's hand still attached.

In front of the house the other four waited tensely once the explosions began. Forty seconds later five Russians dashed from the house, two carrying the Little General computer and three brandishing automatics. The computer was thrust into the back seat beside Gadgets. One Russian followed the computer into the back seat, another jumped in front, barking harsh orders at Pol. Pol didn't need to understand Russian to know what was expected; he powered the car away from the curb. Ahead of him, Lao already had the other Zil careening down the street.

Lao followed her instinct, steering in the general direction of the Russian consulate. At first Esenin was too busy watching for pursuit to notice where they went. When he did notice, he barked something in Russian. When there was no appreciable reaction he swung his Pistole M to cover Lao.

"Too late," Lao said in English. "We're being stopped by Yugoslav troops."

Directly ahead troops were hastily barricading the street. Lao brought the car to a lurching stop right between the muzzles of two AKs, held by determined-looking men in Yugoslav army uniforms.

From the back seat, sandwiched between two KGB goons, Vanessa said in English, "They're not Yugoslavs."

19

Stefan Barazov believed in being prepared for all contingencies, including the risk that the KGB would forget to pay him. He prepared thoroughly before he sent a message to Esenin, telling him where to pick up the computer.

He was especially nervous when he failed to hear that the two trucks had crossed the frontier into Bulgaria. That the Yugoslavs would successfully stop the trucks was always a slim possibility. That was the reason he had not sent the computer on the cross-country trek. It was much safer to turn it over to the Russians and let them take it out of Yugoslavia. They would pay the full fee for the computer, whether the rest of the operation was a success or not.

His precaution was simple, daring and in keeping with his thinking. He had kept ten Bulgarian guards with him and had sent twenty more out in Yugoslav army uniforms. Had the KGB taken the computer without paying, Barazov would not have given the "okay" signal to his disguised troops. They would have stopped the Russians and taken the computer back. If that would have happened, Barazov would have felt free to double the price. Not only would the Soviets have paid, but they would have given him grudging respect and more assignments. That was how things were in the world of Soviet-backed terrorism.

Barazov had known Esenin and his men were coming in two limousines to his villa. Esenin was allowed to approach Barazov's safehouse only through the terrorist's indulgence. That made the Bulgarian terrorist grin with a sense of power. When the six Russians had entered the ground floor, they had been discreetly covered by Bulgarian terrorists. Barazov and Esenin had met in a large front room on the first floor.

Esenin's first words were "You weren't supposed to take any prisoners except the Soviet comrades."

Barazov shrugged. Esenin was looking for a bargaining point, and they both knew it.

Esenin walked over to the computer and opened the top and checked to make sure all the components were there. "Your trucks didn't make it."

"I suspected as much when I hadn't heard. What happened?"

Esenin described the trucks' plunge into the river. "Colonel Obilich handled the entire matter himself. He's still on the scene looking for bodies. It's unsatisfactory," the Russian said. "We cannot pay full price for sloppy work."

Barazov shrugged. "Then you need pay nothing."

"What!"

"We can sell the computer back to the Americans at a profit. I'm letting you have it at the agreed price only because I honor my agreements."

Whatever hot reply Esenin made was lost in the series of explosions that shook the house. Barazov whirled to bark commands to his men. When he turned back, he was covered by the Russian's guns as they backed from the room.

"Not without paying," Barazov yelled.

"We will settle at a less dangerous time," Esenin said just before he broke for the door.

Most of Barazov's men had rushed to the back of the house to fend off the major attack. Those remaining in the front rooms managed to kill only one escaping Russian.

Barazov ordered his men to two cars he had waiting to pursue the Russians, if that became necessary. They poured out the front door in time to see Esenin's two Zils disappear around a corner. A few seconds later he saw an American van speed after them. Barazov and his six remaining men jumped into the two waiting cars and headed after the Russians. So the Russian pig farmer had created the diversion in order to steal the computer. Now he'd pay. The roadblock was only two streets away.

GADGETS DIDN'T WASTE TIME, but he did waste the Russian in the back seat the moment the car started. He brought a silenced 93-R from beside his thigh and splattered the man's brains on the side window. He shifted the weapon and messed up the front window, just to keep things balanced. He fished under his clothing for the needed supplies and started working on the computer.

When Politician was forced to slow the car, Gadgets asked, "What's doing?" without looking up.

"Yugoslav troops have blocked the road. They're covering us with heavy firepower.

"Back up. Vanessa couldn't have arranged this."

"Too late."

Gadgets frantically stuffed things back into his pockets.

Politician bought precious seconds by jumping from the driver's seat and bellowing, "What's the meaning of this?" The guns and attention shifted briefly to the crazy North American, but he wasn't holding a weapon, and the tension subsided. By that time Gadgets had also left the car.

Someone barked orders at them in Russian.

"What's he saying?" Gadgets asked Pol.

"I think we're supposed to give them the computer."

Gadgets gestured to the back seat of the car.

Esenin and another Russian climbed from the first car and started talking rapidly in Russian to someone on the roadblock. Whatever he said didn't cut any ice with the troops who kept their AKs trained on them.

WHEN VANESSA GAVE HER WARNING from the back seat, Lao's hand dropped to her belt. Esenin, temporarily distracted by Vanessa's shout, didn't notice. However, one of the KGB agents in the back seat noticed and thrust his Makarov into the back of Lao's ear. She calmly jammed her communicator button on transmit and brought her hand back to the wheel.

"Everyone out," Esenin commanded in English.

Lao was relieved to get the communicator outside the metal shielding of the car. She climbed out quickly. Vanessa, who had to wait until the Russians were out, followed more slowly.

"They're Bulgarians in disguise, aren't they?" Lao said in a loud voice.

A terrorist, dressed as a Yugoslav artillery captain, slapped her across the mouth.

"Speak when spoken to," he commanded in rough English. Then he turned to Esenin, using English—the common language of terrorism—to communicate with him. "I think you forgot to finish negotiating for the computer."

"I didn't have time. The villa was under attack. Tell the Shrew he will receive full payment before we move any farther." Esenin pointed at Lao then Vanessa then over to Pol and Gadgets. "But kill these four right now. They work for the Americans."

WHEN LYONS SAW THE ROADBLOCK he followed his battle instincts, stopped the van, slipped on a bandoleer of magazines for the Konzak and put his assault shotgun in the seat beside him. He had the special van radio tuned to the EVA frequency. As he put the van into gear once more, Lao's comment came through loud and clear. Lyons thrust the accelerator to the floor before he heard Esenin's command to kill.

He aimed the van at the uniforms closest to the stopped cars. The vehicle slammed into four terrorists, tossing them to either side. Then Lyons simultaneously hit the remote release for the van's side door and stomped on the brakes; the side door flew open. Lyons grabbed the Konzak and jumped out.

Most of the troops were to the left of the van. The Konzak roared a full seven-round magazine on full automatic in that direction. Traveling at 366 meters per second, 350 number-two and double-ought steel balls pulverized human flesh. Those closest to the deadly roar were chopped to pieces. Miscellaneous hands, arms and chunks of chopped flesh showered those who were behind and wildly attempting to dodge the shower of death.

Lyons jammed in a fresh clip and rounded the van in search of more terrorists.

When the van had appeared, Esenin ran for the car containing the computer, shouting to his two remaining Russian helpers.

Pol had moved away from the driver's open door in an attempt to keep eyes focused on himself while Gadgets completed whatever he was doing with the computer. Seconds later Gadgets emerged from the car and stepped away with his hands in the air.

When the van had rammed the Bulgarian terrorists, Pol and Gadgets dived amidst their captors, where it would be most difficult for the Bulgarians to shoot without hitting one another. Suddenly the enemy found their weapons more hindrance than help.

Pol seized a wrist and tugged, pulling an AK forward to jam into the chest of a terrorist beside him. His other hand slammed into the gunman's trigger finger. It set off a short burst that blew the chest out of the man in front of the barrel.

The gunman was so startled when Pol forced him to shoot a comrade that he yanked his hand away from the Kalashnikov as if it had burned him. Pol grabbed the weapon and reversed it. Then it burned the gunman. It burned two more before the bolt fell on an empty chamber.

Ducking, Gadgets placed his hands on the ground and kicked his feet straight out behind him. He knocked two men off their feet, breaking the knee of one. Then, pulling his feet beneath him, he delivered two hard jabs. Each connected with a crotch, causing two more terrorists to lose their concentration on the fight.

While Pol and Gadgets were thus engaged, Esenin and his companions dove into the unattended car. The motor was still idling. Esenin slammed it into gear and stomped on the accelerator. Two more Bulgarians were flattened by the charging Zil as it charged ahead, and the third was hit by the open rear door. The door broke off; it and the terrorist ended up in the gutter together. The Zil bumped over two more bodies then was in the clear. It skidded around a corner, scraping a front fender in testimony to Esenin's anxiety to leave.

Lyons moved in to help Lao, but he saw that she was doing just fine. Grabbing the wrist of a nearby terrorist, she swooped down with her arms then brought them up in a huge circle, jerking the guy off balance. Lao suddenly jerked back and sent her victim whirling into two of his fellow blood merchants. She moved right in behind him, her small but able fists slashing out to crush a pair of Adam's apples.

Standing calmly in the midst of the fray, Vanessa pulled her Model 70 from shoulder leather and took a two-handed firing stance. Four terrorists received two rounds each from her automatic. When she looked up from her sights, there was no one left to shoot.

Seeing that Vanessa needed no assistance, Lyons thundered around the end of the van but found a distinct lack of targets.

Vanessa calmly put a new clip in her Zastava. Then she walked to the van and freshened the original clip from Able Team's supply of parabellums.

"The KGB is getting away with the computer," she reminded Able Team.

With calm efficiency the team members clambered back into the van. They attended to their weapons. Politician slid into the driver's seat and started after the Zil.

"I think the Bulgarian reinforcements are coming up behind us," he said calmly.

Busy with his radio gear, Gadgets reported. "Our pet KGB agent hasn't lost his bug."

Lyons clambered over the seats until he was riding sideways in the back of the van. The Konzak was still in his hand. "Let me know when he's close," he told Pol.

Gadgets told Vanessa which direction their quarry was taking. She translated the information into left- and right-turn instructions for Pol.

"The scum behind us is getting closer," Pol announced.

"Close enough?" Lyons sounded eager.

"Not yet."

Autofire rattled off the armored back of the van. Lyons unlatched the back door and held it shut.

"Not yet," Pol repeated. "Civilians around."

Another burst of fire rattled the van like hail on a tin roof.

"Clear street ahead," Vanessa reported.

Pol started the countdown, slowing the van as he did so. "Five...four...three...two...one...Now!"

Lyons kicked open the back door. A Moskvitch and a Ziguli were in hot pursuit with gunmen hanging out the windows and firing.

Lyons calmly lined up the Konzak and swept a three-shell burst across the windshield of the Ziguli. The heads of the two terrorists in the front seat sprayed blood over those in the back. The small car veered in front of the Moskvitch.

The Moskvitch had to swerve to avoid being run off the road. Lyons held the trigger on autofire and put the rest of the clip through the side windows of the second car. The car swerved behind a building and did not reappear.

As Lyons fastened the rear door and rammed home a fresh clip, Vanessa said, "There's no doubt. They head for the old harbor. They will get there first."

"Not to worry," Gadgets told her.

"We go through Ploce Gate, straight ahead," she told Pol.

In the gathering darkness, the water of the old harbor was deep purple. Roughly two hundred small craft rode at anchor in the lee of the breakwater. The lights of the old town across the water danced on the slow swell in the sheltered harbor.

The Russian Zil stopped at the edge of the water. Esenin and one helper carried the computer to a small motorboat. Standing in 2-1/2 feet of water, a third Russian steadied the boat with his left hand while with his right he pointed a Tokarev TT-33 at a family of four tourists who cowered in the bow.

Lyons threw open the rear door of the van and hung his head below the bumper. Satisfied that the slope of the ground prevented the Russians from shooting his ankles under the van, Lyons climbed out, keeping the armored vehicle between himself and them.

Esenin called out from the water, "If you come closer, Yugoslavia will lose four tourists. Swiss, I think. They spend much money here."

"We're not suckers," Lyons shouted. "You take them with you, and they're dead meat, too. You can either surrender or die. It makes no difference to the hostages whether you or I kill them."

Esenin wanted no part of this frigid avenger. The KGB man knew that his only hope was to trade the hostages for his life.

"Don't be hasty," Esenin yelled, struggling to keep the panic from his voice. "I'm willing to guarantee the safety of these people, if we are allowed to leave."

"Horse shit."

Esenin didn't consider that a promising reply. He tried again, "Perhaps you can suggest a way out of this situation?"

There was a long pause while the KGB killer tasted his own mortality.

Finally Lyons answered, his voice still frigid and hinting at a barely suppressed anger. "Take them to the near side of the breakwater. Head for any place other than the nearest point, and I'll blast you. Have them stand in a row on the edge of the breakwater. Use them as a screen as you move out to sea."

Esenin thought it over. It seemed a workable idea. A frigate waited out in the Adriatic. It was improbable that air support could arrive on the scene before the motorboat reached the ship. If he could keep this madman from killing him, he'd make it. Esenin looked again at Lyons's face, barely visible past the edge of the van. The face held a ferocious scowl.

"We will do as you say," Esenin called. He pushed the computer onto the deck and then heaved himself on board. The other Russians climbed aboard and stowed the computer more safely.

Esenin could scarcely retain his glee. He was going to live. He was also going to return to Russia with one of the West's most advanced computers.

"One wrong move, and you're blasted out of the water," Lyons grated.

The motorboat moved slowly to the breakwater. Standing side by side, the family formed a human shield for the escaping KGB operatives. Esenin decided against shooting them. There was a good chance those American warriors had rifles that could still blast him out of the water. By the time he was out of rifle range, the hostages would be out of pistol range.

But just before he gunned the boat away, Esenin could not resist a triumphant laugh.

"So long, suckers," he called.

As the motorboat headed straight out into the Adriatic, Vanessa left the van and stood beside Lyons.

"I know it was hard for you, but thank you for saving those lives. I thought no one could negotiate their safety."

Lyons watched the retreating boat. Light was fading quickly now; the vessel was merely a dark mass on the water.

Lyons raised his voice slightly. "Gadgets, give the lady the honor."

Gadgets approached. "How do you know I managed it? I had only ninety seconds alone in the back seat of the car."

"You're Able Team. You managed. Give the lady the box."

Gadgets handed a box the size of a cigarette package to Vanessa. It sported an aerial and a red button.

"Press the button," Lyons told her.

Vanessa nodded and pushed the button with her thumb. The darkness over the water was lit by a red flash, then a rumbling boom rolled to their ears.

"How did you manage that?" asked Vanessa, looking incredulously first at Gadgets and then at Lyons.

"It was easy. Gadgets put C-4—an explosive—and a radio detonator in the computer."

"Brilliant," said Vanessa, shaking her head.

"Let's move!" Lyons shouted. "We've a plane to catch."

VANESSA ACCOMPANIED THEM to the airport and made her goodbyes there.

Able Team's van rolled into the Hercules the moment the last pallet of cargo was forklifted off. Jack Grimaldi was there to greet Able Team and the four chess masters.

"Jack, why would you be flying this buggy?" Pol asked.

"I like these old planes. Besides, I've got something much faster waiting in Athens. Brognola needs you in Washington, soonest."

"We still have a batch of dirt called the Gun Team to take care of," Lyons said.

"Yeah," Gadgets chimed in. "We still don't know why they were trying to eliminate the entire American chess team."

"Hal needs you" was Grimaldi's entire argument.

"What's up," Lyons demanded.

"Some sort of super hitmen are knocking off some VIPs. All the bigwigs in D.C. are having shit hemorrhages. Hal needs you before a lot of it gets dumped on him."

Lyons turned to the rest of the team. "Grab shut-eye. We're going to need it."

AVAILABLE NOW!

Following the success of Dirty War comes SuperBolan #5

A routine flight departing Munich for New York is forced to land at Beirut International Airport.

A whispered word echoes through the jumbo's cabin, leaving panic and terror in its wake.

Hijack!

Aboard the giant silver bird the occupants silently await their fate.

And among them is a special passenger. . . .

MORE ACTION!
MORE SUSPENSE!
NEW LOOK!

THE EXECUTIONER

MACK BOLAN

Beginning in July, watch out for America's number-one hero, Mack Bolan, in more spectacular, more gut-wrenching missions.

The Executioner continues to live large in bigger, bolder stories that can only be told in 256 pages.

Get into the heart of the man and the heart of the action with the first big entry, **The Trial**.

In this gripping adventure, Bolan is captured and placed on trial for his life—accused by the government he had sworn to serve. And the prosecution is hunting for the soldier's head.

Gold Eagle Books is giving readers what they asked for. You've never read action-adventure like this before!

Take
4 explosive books
plus a
mystery bonus
FREE